A Pimby Tale

Adventures into Imagination

Robert Pardi

www.robertpardi.com

A Pimby Tale

Adventures into Imagination

A Pimby Tale, Adventures into Imagination
by Robert Pardi

Illustrations by Julia Alcoba

ISBN-13: 978-1-988925-94-3
First Edition   Printed in the United States of America

PROMINENCE
PUBLISHING

Available on Amazon

It is a happy talent to know how to play.

Ralph Waldo Emerson

Author's Welcome Note

Welcome to the land of Pimbies, a magical world of imagination.

The idea for this modern-day fable bubbled up after my first visit to India. It was while sitting on the floor of a magnificent temple that many of the lessons I've learned throughout my life echoed in my mind, literally asking to be shared. Yet, there were many starts and stops in creating this book. Something was blocking the flow.

What happened next now seems like magical intervention. I started to dream about my own childhood, and my long-forgotten imaginary friend named Filbert. I'd wake up smiling. During the day I'd ponder the wondrous adventures he and I had embarked upon, how he had offered me advice on how to deal with certain, difficult childhood situations. The dam broke and the book flowed forth.

It became obvious to me that this book had to merge what I believe are important lessons to contemplate, honestly at any age, with the voice of Filbert. Hence, A Pimby Tale was born.

I dedicate this
To the dreamer in all of us.
To those who believe in possibilities.
To those who yearn to expand, stretch, and grow.
To those who wish to see things differently.
To my beautiful Grandmother Fella
who taught me to live life freely,
and never be afraid to dream and take chances.
And finally, to my forever love Desiree
who will always be my muse.

I am a big believer that we should always maintain our childlike enthusiasm for life. That we should look forward with enthusiasm and curiosity to the wonder of life. That we should never lose our connection to play and the power of imagination, something that sadly happens all too often as we age.

Storytelling is extremely important to our sense of connection and belonging. My dream is that adults will read A Pimby Tale with their children and grandchildren and discuss the lessons that will help them stay connected to their inner child.

Join me in play. Be free, be open, be curious and enjoy your journey into the land of Pimbies.

If you want your children to be smart,
tell them stories.
If you want them to be really smart,
tell them more stories.
If you want your children to be brilliant,
tell them even more stories.

Albert Einstein

Acknowledgments

Writing this book was more rewarding that I could have ever imagined. The seed of this story was born through the experiences my wife and I experienced while in India as well as during her journey with terminal breast cancer. We dreamed of how it would have been nice to tell such stories to the children we were destined not to have because of her illness. I decided to write this tale because I could no longer contain it in my heart.

None of this would have been possible without the love of my wife Desiree who remains a beautiful gemstone in the mosaic of my life. I am eternally grateful to my Grandmother Fella who taught me the value of curiosity and to approach life with childlike enthusiasm.

I'm also forever indebted to Trish Laub, Kamie Lehmann, and Brenda Blais Nesbitt for their unwavering support and keen insights in helping me bring this story to life.

A very special, heartfelt thanks to Phyllis Melhado who had the faith in me that I could become an author. If not for her, I would not have been able to publish my first book Chasing Life.

A big thank you to all those who have been a part of my getting to this stage of my life, including my imaginary friend who, when I was eight years old, helped me through tough times. I am grateful to the many true, authentic people I have met through the years. And, for my cousin Julia Alcoba, I have the warmest thanks for bringing the characters of Johnny and Filbert to life through her artistic talents.

Finally, a thank you to those of you who have purchased this book. May modern-day fable inspire the inner child in you to live a wholehearted life.

Contents

Imagination is more important than knowledge. For knowledge is limited to all we now know and understand, while Imagination embraces the entire world, and all there ever will be to know and understand.

Albert Einstein

The Encounter

Johnny turned over in his bed for the third or fourth time. The ongoing heatwave in his small town made him restless. It was not only the hottest night in Hopewell Junction's history but would also turn out to be the night that would change Johnny's life forever.

"Uffa. 1:08 a.m.," he grumbled, frustrated, eyeing the clock. I'm never going to get any sleep tonight."

Despite the fan whirling at full blast, his room felt like a sizzling pizza oven.

"I wish my folks would turn up the AC and not worry so much about the planet," he mumbled, while fluffing his pillow to get more comfortable.

Oddly, it wasn't only the heat that was keeping Johnny awake. There was this strange sound, like a huge machine humming somewhere nearby, but he couldn't figure out where it was coming from.

He fluffed his pillow once more, hoping for a cooler spot in a losing battle against the heat, when suddenly, he heard, "Psst… Psst."

Johnny wiggled his ear with his little finger, telling himself the sound was just his imagination.

A few seconds later, he heard it again, "Psst…Psst."

This time he hopped out of bed to check out what was going on. When Johnny was younger, he used to believe monsters hid in his room. Now, despite being older, he couldn't believe that he still felt a little scared.

"There are no such things as monsters. That's kids' stuff. You are almost nine years old," he whispered to himself. Then, he took a deep breath, stood tall, and scanned the room.

The light of a big, bright, full moon shone through his window, like a spotlight. This made it easy for him to look around without having to turn on the light. He remembered how, up until about two years ago, he'd always stare out his window at the full moon before going to bed. He loved full moons, mostly because his dad used to tell him that the bright moonbeams carried lots of magic down to earth. That was before his dad started working so much and still had time to tell him bedtime stories. Now, unfortunately, he rarely saw his father before going to sleep.

"It's on the night of a bright full moon," his dad told him, "when it seems almost as bright as daytime, that all the magical beings come out to play because they're energized by this very special, rare type of light."

Johnny laughed to himself - he hadn't thought about that in a long time.

"This is silly," he told himself. "I'm making a big deal over some little noise that I'm probably just imagining anyway."

Just then, from the corner of his eye, Johnny noticed something by the giant, spooky maple tree outside his window. When his family first moved in, that tree got zapped by lightning, leaving a scary mark on the branch right near Johnny's window. He always thought that branch looked like a huge, creepy snake. And for almost a whole year after the lightning hit, he'd have nightmares about it coming alive and trying to gobble him up.

2

Squinting his eyes from afar, Johnny tried to figure out what that thing near the tree was. But, oh boy, it was way too far for him to see clearly! All he could tell was that it was pretty tiny.

What could it be?

He crept nearer to the window to get a better look at the strange shape, using his hands like binoculars to block the bright moonlight from his eyes. The funny object shimmered, constantly changing colors, like a kaleidoscope. Just then it seemed to hop forward. Johnny dropped down below the window because he feared scaring it away.

What could it be?

He slowly stood up and tried to focus his eyes solely on the object. It appeared to have the shape of a chipmunk, but as soon as he clearly focused on it, poof, it vanished. He strained his eyes searching for the object, but only the glimmering moonlight remained dancing on the dewy grass.

A bunch of ideas popped into his mind about what it might have been as he stumbled back to bed.

It must've been a candy wrapper reflecting the moonlight. Maybe a piece of glass in the grass or a piece of aluminum foil that blew out of the garbage pail? Yeah, nothing more than a piece of aluminum foil.

After climbing back under the covers, he noticed that the strange humming sound had also stopped.

Johnny convinced himself that the sound was probably a piece of paper or maybe even a leaf that had gotten caught in the fan and finally blew free. He rubbed his eyes, stretched his arms, let out a great big yawn, and fell fast asleep.

Later that morning, he heard his mother yelling his name from the bottom of the stairs.

"Johnny, Johnny...Johnny! Get down here right now! You know what time I have to be at work! Where is your head young man?"

Johnny jumped up in his bed as if someone had poked him with a needle. He quickly got dressed and flew down the stairs – almost knocking over his nanny, Ms. Cathy Carefree. When he reached the bottom of the stairs, his mother was tapping her watch with her index finger.

Johnny opened his mouth to say something, but his mother didn't give him a chance.

"I've told you time and time again young man, this world does not like laziness. I've been down here for ages waiting for you. You know when I need to leave for the hospital, right? Don't you care about the sick people Mommy has to take care of? Don't you realize they need me? Don't you realize how important my being a doctor is for other people?"

"Uh-oh," was the only word Johnny could say before his mother started speaking again.

"Hush Johnny," his mother said in a firm voice. "I want you to pay close attention - Cathy knows the schedule I set for you today. It's almost mid-July and time to finish your summer fun. You need to start preparing yourself for the next school year."

"But Mom, the summer is just getting started," Johnny whined.

"You don't have playtime when you are an adult, so you might as well get used to it now!" Johnny's mother roared as if Johnny was still upstairs.

"But why? Why is there no fun time when I get older?"

"Because that is the way it is, Johnny. Get used to it. Now I don't have any more time for this nonsense talk. Listen to Cathy and go brush your teeth."

"Wait. Dad said I could ask you about my birthday party. He said nine is a really special birthday."

"Later," was all Mrs. Prospect said before dashing out the door.

After gobbling down his breakfast, Johnny dashed across the street to his buddy Mickey Dakota's place. Johnny and Mickey were almost the same age—just nine weeks apart! Even though they looked different, lots of people thought they could be brothers. Their families had Italian and Irish roots.

Johnny was tall and skinny with wavy black hair, a big nose, olive skin, and these huge brown eyes that looked like chocolate. On the other hand, Mickey was a tad shorter and slightly stockier, with straight brown hair, lighter skin, and eyes that were this cool mix of green and brown.

Johnny's mom was really pretty and kind of short, just 5 feet and 2 inches tall. She had long, shiny blonde hair, blue eyes that sparkled, and a smile that made everyone say, 'Wow!' His dad, who worked in banking, was about 5'8" and super fit. You could tell he was Italian from his dark skin, black hair, and big, dark eyes.

Mickey's dad was a police officer and super Irish-looking with bright red hair, freckles everywhere, and these cool green eyes. He was so tall and strong, almost like a basketball player! He was the captain of the police force in Hopewell Junction. Mickey's mom, with her super curly black hair and light brown eyes, was really tiny - she wasn't even 5 feet tall! She looked after Mickey and his siblings, Billy, Tommy, and Suzie, instead of working.

It used to be a summer tradition for Mickey and Johnny to visit a different place on their bikes each day, but lately, Johnny preferred spending more and more time inside, either on his computer or playing video games. This summer he found himself preferring the electronic fantasy world much more than Hopewell Junction.

"Hey, Mickey, nine weeks to my birthday!"

"Man Johnny, what are you going to do, count down every day for me?"

"Yeah, I think I will. My dad says the ninth birthday is a super important one."

"Why?" Mickey asked.

"I really don't know, but he said so and I believe him."

"Well, I bet you get a dynamite gift."

"I'm just hoping both my parents will be here for my birthday this year. Remember last year when my dad had to go away on business during my birthday?"

"Oh yeah, I forgot, but you did get that mind-blowing video game system."

"Yeah, but I would have said no to any present just to have him home. Anyway, my mom only gave me two hours for playtime today. What do you want to do?"

"Really? Only two hours? That's nuts. I seriously don't understand parents," Mickey said, crossing his eyes.

"Me neither," Johnny responded.

"How about a quick bike ride? We haven't gone on one in like forever and it's a great day for a ride."

"Boring! Where'd we even go?"

"Hmm, maybe Crooked Creek Falls?" Mickey suggested.

"Aw, come on Mick! That's for little kids. We've been there a zillion times! What about hanging and playing the car racing video game my dad bought me last week?"

"You're kidding right? The falls are awesome. Remember last year? Now we're big enough to go alone, no big brother Billy needed! Plus, we can save video games for winter. Today is a perfect day for a bike ride. Come on."

"I don't know, Mickey."

"Well, there's only one way to decide what to do and that means it's going to come down to 3-2-1."

Mickey whipped out a water gun from his back pocket and before Johnny could grab his own, SPLASH! Johnny's shirt was soaked. Whenever they couldn't decide what to do in the summer, they'd duel with water pistols, and the winner got to choose.

"Ha, I guess you are getting old Johnny, and it's made you slow – very slow," Mickey joked.

"That's not fair Mickey. I wasn't prepared," Johnny said with a sulky look on his face.

"Crooked Creek it is, you know the rules, Johnny. Winner's choice."

Johnny, head now held low, nodded in agreement.

They hopped onto their bikes and made their way to Crooked Creek Falls. It had always been one of Johnny's favorite spots because, almost every day, the mist from the falls made a rainbow. Johnny's dad used to tell him tales about how rainbows were made from the light of magical beings playing near the falls.

He and his dad used to visit often, before his dad got really busy. He remembered how they'd pack a big lunch, climb to the highest rock they could reach, lay out a blanket, and watch the falls while they ate. And whenever a rainbow appeared, Mr. Prospect would whisper to Johnny about colorful energy from creatures called "Pimbies."

It was nearly 10 a.m. when Johnny and Mickey finally arrived at the falls. They couldn't believe their eyes that the big thermometer in the park had already reached a whopping 90 degrees.

"Mickey, I can't believe it's this hot already!"

"Me neither. Good thing the water's cold."

"You know I can't go in the water. My mom would be so upset if I got these clothes dirty, and I didn't bring a bathing suit or a towel."

"Dude, we can put our feet in like we used to do. Come on, it is so hot!"

"Mickey, she told me I have to start taking better care of my clothes because when we grow up and are in the real world, we can't walk around with dirty clothes. So, I can't. What if muddy water splashes on my shorts? She will harp on me if she finds out I came home with my clothes dirty."

"You're kidding, right? So, you don't want to hunt for turtles or frogs, or maybe play soldiers?"

"No Mickey, really - I can't get dirty! See, that is why this place is for kids. It's ok for kids to get dirty, but I can't! My mom says you never know who you're going to meet, and we should always look nice."

"All right bro. Don't know which important person we could meet, who knows, maybe a famous actor who decided to come to the falls," Mickey snickered.

Mickey then caught the big frown on Johnny's face and said, "Bro, don't get mad. Come on, we can find many fun things to do without getting dirty. What about skipping rocks across the pond at the end of the creek? Does that sound cool?"

"Yeah, thanks man. It's just my mom has really been on my case about getting ready for the real world."

"Dude, I don't understand the difference between this world and the real world, but I'm sure all of our parents are totally wacko."

"Yeah," Johnny chuckled. "I don't get it either Mickey, but my mom says parents know best."

Mickey and Johnny walked down a dirt path to where the falls emptied into a small pond. They were super surprised that no one else was swimming, even though it was crazy hot! But hey, having the whole pond to themselves was awesome.

Johnny reached for a smooth rock to skip on the water when he noticed something shiny on the other side of the lake. For an instant, it looked just like what he'd seen outside his window earlier that morning. He squinted, trying to get a better look, but it vanished in a flash.

"What are you staring at?" Mickey asked.

"Aww, nothing. Just thought I saw something across the lake. That reminds me, I've got to tell you about the weirdest thing that happened last night. I'm sure it was just my imagination, but it was so bizarre."

Johnny told Mickey everything - the weird humming, the strange creature he thought he saw outside his window, and how he ended up thinking it was all just his imagination.

"Whoa, that's crazy! What do you think it really was? Will it come back? Maybe it was one of those magical things your dad mentioned. What were they called again?"

"Pimbies," Johnny responded.

"Yeah, a Pimby!"

"Impossible Mickey, there are no such things as Pimbies. He totally made all that up. I told you it was a candy wrapper or something, but nothing magical. I'm sure it was nothing magical," Johnny said with his face getting a bit red. "There are no such things as Pimbies!"

"Johnny, no need to sound angry, but come on – maybe it was. Why not believe it, right?" Mickey asked. "What if I sleep over and we can play detective and see if it comes back? That would be so awesome. We haven't had a sleepover in a long time."

"Mickey, I'm telling you it really was nothing. I knew not to tell you. Now you are getting all looney, but as I told you - Pimbies don't exist! It's impossible they're real. They can't be! If they were, wouldn't they teach us about them in school?"

"I guess you're right. Anyway, it's still fun to pretend."

"My mom says pretending is a waste of time." Suddenly Johnny panicked, "Oh man, what time is it?"

"It's almost noon. You have to get back, right?"

"Yeah, I have to go shopping with Cathy to get some clothes for the next school year, and I also have to do some math," Johnny said with a long face.

"Yuck! Math? Bummer!"

"I know, I know, but I have to," Johnny said with a deep sigh. "My mom insists that I do some each day because I only got a B+ last year in Math."

"Ok, let's go. We can peddle super-fast and get back before you get in trouble."

As they rode, Johnny stayed quiet. He started wondering what if Pimbies were real. *They can't be,* he thought, pedaling hard to keep up with Mickey. Yet, he couldn't shake the feeling that something had been outside his window. He also had a strange feeling that something had been following him since he'd woken up and tried to brush it off.

"It's just my imagination playing tricks on me," he kept saying to himself over and over.

My Name is Filbert

"**M**om, do you think Dad will get home before I have to go to bed? I haven't seen him in almost a week."

"Why Johnny, do you have something important you need to talk to him about?"

"No, not really Mom. I just wanted to ask him a little bit more about Pimbies."

"Oh, for heaven's sake. I told your father it was a waste of time telling you those ridiculous stories. Now he's filled your head with garbage!" his mother snapped.

"You are almost nine years old, and it's high time you put away childish thoughts. Plus, your father has been incredibly busy, and I'm sure he doesn't want to be bothered with such silliness when he has time to relax."

"Sorry, Mom, I just well, never mind. Can I go over to Mickey's for a little while?"

"Just be back by 9 p.m."

"Thanks."

Johnny ran across the street to Mickey's house. All the homes on Wishing Well Lane were similar. They all had two floors, a two-car garage, and shutters on the windows. But Mickey's house was special. It sat right on top of this big hill. It was awesome for sledding whenever it snowed!

Johnny first met Mickey when they were both five years old. Johnny's parents moved to Hopewell Junction to get away from the hustle and bustle of the big city. Johnny never understood why. Johnny always thought the city was super cool. Every Christmas since they moved there, he begged to go see the city all lit up.

His mom, for some reason, didn't like the city very much, so it was always his dad who took him to see the extravagant Christmas decorations. They'd head straight for the giant Christmas tree in the middle of town. Then, their next stop was Frosty's, this ice cream place high up on the 81st floor of the tallest building in the world. It was like stepping into a neon wonderland, with chairs that looked like giant marshmallows.

They ordered the same thing every year - Frosty's super-duper banana split with star-shaped sprinkles and two hot chocolates with loads of whipped cream. He loved those times with his father who would tell him all kinds of stories about magic and how wishes do come true.

While sitting down on the curb outside Mickey's house, he started to daydream about the first time they went to Frosty's. He remembered how he'd pressed himself up against the big windows facing outwards toward the city and stretched his arms in the shape of a T.

"What are you doing Johnny?" his father asked.

"I'm seeing what it would be like to fly like a bird, Dad. The cars and people are so tiny from way up here. This is what it must look like to birds."

"You're so right, Johnny, and do you want to know a secret?"

"Yeah, what?" Johnny answered in such a loud excited voice that other customers turned to stare at him.

"That's just how the airplane was invented. Two brothers wondered what it would be like to fly like a bird. Soon they started to pretend and imagine how birds flew and then, after heaps of hard work, they built the first airplane. They figured it out first by imagining it and then by building it. Thanks to them, we can all fly to many places all around the world and even out in space because they used their imagination."

"Really, Dad? That's so cool."

"Yes, really Johnny. Imagination is enormously powerful and incredibly magical. Everything is first created in imagination, Johnny. The shoes you are wearing, the building we are in, even the delicious banana split we are eating. Imagination is the land of the Pimbies, magical creatures who teach us we are Possibility in …."

Just then Johnny got pulled out of his daydream by a water balloon bursting right next to his leg.

"Johnny, are you going to hang out on the curb the whole night? I thought you fell asleep! What were you thinking about?"

"Hey, Mickey. I was thinking about my dad. He's been super busy lately. I don't even get the chance to say hi to him anymore. He does leave me cool notes though, but you know, I miss talking with him."

"That stinks", Mickey said. "Did you leave him a note about that night you thought you saw something out your window?"

"Nah, I wanted to, but the more I thought about it, the more it seemed totally lame. Plus, I didn't want to waste his time because he's always so busy. I'm sure he only told me those stupid Pimby stories as make believe – you know, 'pretend stuff.' Anyway, whatever it was hasn't come back. So, case closed."

"I guess, Johnny," Mickey said sounding a little upset. He felt sad that Johnny didn't get to hang out with his dad like he did with his own.

"Well, Johnny, I have a surprise for you. Listen to this! My dad still has some sparklers left over from 4th of July. He said he'd light them for us, and my mom said we can make s'mores!"

"YUM! Count me in," said Johnny as his stomach started to grumble.

Mr. and Mrs. Dakota were always super friendly to Johnny as were Mickey's two brothers and older sister. Their house was like a busy train station. People were constantly coming and going, and the house was always filled with lots of noise and laughter. Mickey's grandparents, Nanny and Gramps, also lived on the bottom floor. Nanny, a tiny Italian woman, was always cooking up meatballs, so the bottom floor smelled like an Italian restaurant. Gramps, from Napoli, was always sitting in his comfy, big recliner, reading the newspaper while waiting patiently for Nanny's cooking.

"Delizioso" was one of the first words Nanny taught Johnny, which means "delicious" in Italian. Johnny loved hanging out at Mickey's house, and Mickey's parents even called him their adopted son, which made him feel super special.

"So, Johnny", began Mr. Dakota, "how's your summer going?"

"Great, Mr. D." Johnny had called Mickey's parents Mr. and Mrs. D from the very first day Johnny and his family moved to Hopewell Junction.

He recalled that day like it was yesterday. The movers had already begun unpacking by the time he and his parents arrived at their new house. Mickey dashed across the street as soon as Johnny stepped out of the car. With a big smile, Mickey grabbed one of the hugest empty boxes he could find and dragged it across the street to his house.

"What are you doing?" Johnny asked.

"I'm going to build our clubhouse in my backyard. Don't you think this box will make a great clubhouse?"

"That's such a great idea," Johnny answered. They'd been best friends ever since.

Johnny remembered how they couldn't stop laughing as they struggled to drag that huge box across the street. That's when Mickey's parents came over to introduce themselves to Johnny's parents. After the grown-ups met, Mr. Dakota approached the boys and helped them move the box to Mickey's backyard. They plopped it under a massive pine tree. Johnny turned to Mr. Dakota and said, "Thank you, sir," with a smile."

"Call me Mr. D. son," Mr. Dakota replied with a wink.

Johnny now thought of Mickey, his parents, and his whole family as his family as well. It made him forget that he was an only child. He even went with them on their annual family camping trip to Slippery Slopes.

Johnny must've devoured six s'mores before he had to head home. He loved chilling on the grass, watching fireflies flicker around. Mr. Dakota handed each boy a sparkler for a final duel in the dark. They waved them like swords until the sparklers fizzled out. Johnny knew it was time to leave, but he really didn't want to. But he didn't want to upset his mom by staying out late again.

As he turned to bid Mr. and Mrs. D. goodnight, he heard a humming sound. At first, he thought it was Mickey's bug zapper. But listening closer, he recognized that same mysterious sound from the other night - the one just before he spotted that strange thing outside his window. Hoping Mickey heard it too, he turned and asked, "Do you hear a humming sound?"

"What are you talking about Johnny? I don't hear anything. I think you're going crazy now that you're getting older. Maybe you're losing your hearing, and I should buy you a hearing aid for your birthday," he roared, laughing uncontrollably at his own joke.

"Yeah, you're right. I think I ate too many s'mores and now have a wicked sugar buzz going on."

They both started to giggle.

"You definitely ate too many," Mickey said, puffing his cheeks out for effect. "You're starting to look like a chipmunk, and your mom is going to yell when she sees how much chocolate you have on your shirt."

"Ugh. I'm absolutely going to hear it, but they were so yummy!"

Johnny said goodnight to everyone and went home. He glanced up at the window of his father's study as he crossed the street, hoping to find his dad home. But the room was dark. Johnny felt a bit sad. Just like always, his dad was working late.

"Hey Mom", Johnny yelled as he walked through the front door. He immediately turned to his right, having heard the jingle of his mom's keys, and found her in the dining room preparing her medical bag.

"Johnny, there's an emergency at the hospital, and I need to rush off. Get straight into bed, ok? I should be home in about one hour," his mother barked while hurrying past him as she left the house.

Johnny felt like he'd gotten punched in the stomach watching his mom run out the door. He now felt incredibly unwanted and was terribly upset that his father hadn't come home yet. He missed him horribly and realized it had been at least a week since they last saw each other. He asked Cathy, his nanny, in a very shaky voice while trying to hold back his tears, if she knew when his father would be home.

"Sorry, Johnny. Your mom told me your dad might have to stay in the city again tonight. He's still working on that big project, and she said he has to give an important presentation extremely early tomorrow morning. It probably wouldn't make sense for him to come home tonight. You understand, right?"

Johnny said nothing. He just lowered his head and started climbing up the stairs.

"Johnny, I know you are sad that he isn't home much recently but look at the positive side - your mother didn't notice all the chocolate on your shirt," Cathy said, joking.

Johnny smiled back. Cathy told him to leave his shirt outside his door so she could wash away the evidence of the s'mores feast.

Thinking of it as "evidence" finally made Johnny laugh out loud and then he turned to her and said, "Thanks Cathy, goodnight."

"Goodnight, Johnny. Sweet dreams."

After tossing his shirt outside the door, he threw himself on the bed and thought about how lucky Mickey was to spend so much time with his father. Around Johnny's sixth birthday, his dad had received a promotion and from that point on had started working lots of overtime.

I never thought he'd be gone so often. I guess I'm getting a little too old to be doing things with my dad anyway, he thought while lying on his back staring at the ceiling. But deep down, he knew he missed his dad tremendously.

Suddenly, the humming sound became so loud he felt like his ears would pop. Startled, he jumped up and rushed out of his room to go ask Cathy if she'd heard it, but as soon as he opened his door, the humming stopped.

This is so weird. I wonder why I'm hearing this sound. Maybe I should tell my mom about it tomorrow? Maybe I have something wrong with my ears, he thought, going back into his room to play video games before going to bed. One of the things he loved about the summer was he could stay up until 10 p.m.

Later that night, he woke up with a fright when the humming sound started again. He glanced at the clock and couldn't believe it was 1:08 a.m., the same exact time the humming sound had woken him up the other night he'd heard it.

Before he even had time to sit up, he heard, "Psst...Psst."
"Oh, this is too weird," he said aloud.

"Psst...Psst," he heard again.

He then hopped out of bed towards the window to see what was making the noise. Unfortunately, he didn't notice his skateboard on the floor and stumbled, stubbing his toe on the dresser.

"Ouch," he said under his breath, not wanting to wake anyone up. He limped over to the window. Once more, that weird thing was under the big maple tree. This time he saw it more clearly because the night was super dark, almost spooky. It looked like a chubby chipmunk, but way bigger. Its face was rounder, and its tail was shorter. The most amazing thing was that it glowed with all the colors of the rainbow. Bright colors, flickering like lights on a Christmas tree.

Oh, this can't be. I must be dreaming or something, he thought.

"My imagination must be playing tricks on me", he whispered under his breath.

"Not exactly," the creature replied.

Stunned, Johnny jumped back from the window and sank down to the floor under the windowsill, desperately searching, deep in his mind, for explanations about what was happening. Finally, he decided that Mickey had probably snuck out of his house to play some sort of trick on him.

Yeah, it must be Mickey, it has to be! He was the only one that I spoke to about this.

He slowly inched up, closer and closer to the windowsill. The closer he got to the open window, the louder the humming became. At one point, it grew so loud that he had to cover his ears and close his eyes. When he opened his eyes, there, floating right outside his window, was the creature, glowing so brightly that his entire bedroom was filled with colorful light, reminding him of the ceiling at Frosty's.

Then, in the most unusual low voice, the creature spoke. "Do not be afraid. Your imagination is not playing tricks on you. In fact, your imagination is working perfectly as I am a piece of your imagination, or what people in your world call 'a figment of imagination.' Soon, you will learn that everything is really a piece of your imagination. Imagination is more powerful than you can possibly believe."

Johnny felt very confused and had no clue what the creature was talking about. But weirdly, its voice also made him feel calm. It reminded him of a peculiar musical instrument his father once had in his study, not something usual like a guitar or trumpet, but more like a big glass bowl. He surprised himself by remembering the bowl because he couldn't have been more than five years old when he saw his dad playing it. Yet, for some reason, in this exact moment, the memory returned crystal clear.

Johnny remembered sitting at the top of the stairs watching his father carry a big, white glass bowl about the size of a beach ball into the living room, where there were many people waiting. The bowl looked like a big, frosted ice cube. He used to like to spy on his dad when he had guests, who usually preferred sitting on the floor with their legs crossed. His father explained to everyone that the bowl was a gift from someone "very important" who lived in a place called Tibet.

Before he'd begun working so much, his dad, who collected globes, would tell Johnny stories about the many different places in the world. Over time, Johnny also grew to love globes and maps. He'd spend hours studying maps, fantasizing about all the places he hoped to visit. That's why, at a young age, he knew that Tibet was located at the top of India, next to China.

He remembered how his father reached into his back pocket and pulled out a small rubber stick, like a tiny baseball bat. Then, his dad lightly tapped the bowl with the mallet. Immediately, the whole house filled with a ringing sound very similar to the church bells he used to hear at the big cathedral in the city near where they lived before moving to Hopewell Junction.

Next, he moved the stick around the outside of the bowl, which created a sound that seemed to shake the whole house. The only other thing he remembered about that night was his father telling his guests, "We are all energy. Now connect to the energy of unlimited possibilities - the possibilities inside your bodies and let your imagination guide you."

How weird that memory popped into my head, Johnny thought. *Why would the sound of this strange creature's voice remind me of that bowl?*

"You can't be real. I don't know how, but I know you are down there Mickey," he whispered from the window so as not to wake his parents.

"I guess it would be easier to believe that Johnny, but I am real, and Mickey is fast asleep in his bed. You will begin to understand more in time. For now, I just wanted to introduce myself. My name is Filbert, and if you are wondering, I am in fact a Pimby."

POP was the last thing Johnny heard before Filbert disappeared, and all that remained was a spooky silence. The humming had stopped. Johnny sat back down on his bed, staring in the direction of the window. He felt frozen and unbelievably baffled about what had just happened.

I wish my dad was home, was all he could think.

He quickly went over to his computer, on a mission to find out everything he could about Pimbies. He remained awake until the crack of dawn, running back and forth from his computer to the window. He didn't find anything on the Internet, not one website nor article - not one single thing about Pimbies.

How could they be real if there isn't anything about them anywhere? It's impossible; Google knows everything. And if Mickey was able to trick me, how did he make the humming sound? How did he make that thing float, and then the sound and the Pimby both disappear instantly, at the same time? And how in the world did he make it talk and glow so brightly?

His head was spinning with questions. But no matter how hard he tried to find answers, nothing made any sense to him. Slowly, as the sun started to rise, Johnny's eyes began to close, and he fell asleep in the chair next to his computer.

Rap…Rap.

Johnny fell off the chair and quickly surveyed the room, squinting his eyes against the brightness of the morning sun.

Rap...Rap, he heard again, immediately flying to the window, thinking his visitor had come back. But as soon as he looked down towards the grass, he saw Mickey standing below with a big branch in his hand that he had used to tap the window.

"Johnny, are you going to sleep in all day? I'm usually the sleepyhead, but, come on dude, it's past 10 a.m. I thought we were going to play your video game this morning. Are you feeling ok?"

"You should know how I'm feeling, Mickey. Great joke last night."

"What are you talking about?"

"You know, one o'clock in the morning, coming over and pretending to have a Pimby outside my window."

"Whoa, no way! It wasn't me. That is so cool! Was it the same thing you saw the other night? Do you think it will come back? This is way too cool! Now you definitely have to let me sleep over, and no way I'm taking 'no' for an answer!" Mickey shouted, all hyped up.

"Come on Mickey, you can't be telling me you didn't pull that stunt last night. It's impossible that thing was real. If it wasn't you, then it must've been a dream."

"Maybe, but it would be fun to try and find out if it is real. Come on, ask your mom if I can sleep over."

"Ok, sure, but you don't really think it's real, do you? Maybe my dad is secretly playing jokes on me like old times?"

"Could be, but we can play detective and find out. Come on, Johnny, we could be like Holmes and Watson."

"Deal! You're right. Let's figure this out. I'll ask my mom if you can sleep over. I'm sure she'll say yes."

A Special Place

Roughly a week had gone by since Johnny met Filbert. Mickey, super excited about meeting a Pimby, had stayed over for three nights in a row. But sadly, nothing strange had happened.

Johnny felt really stupid and kind of embarrassed about having gotten so excited. Now he was sure it must have only been a dream. Yet, the thought that Pimbies somehow existed made him feel closer to his father.

Frustrated, Johnny finally decided that he had no choice but to talk to his dad about everything that had happened. Before going to bed one night, he left his father a note telling him that he really needed to talk with him. He felt bad bothering him because he knew how hard he'd been working. But it was his dad who continually talked about Pimbies, so Johnny needed to understand the truth.

He woke up to find a note taped to his door. "Ok son," his dad wrote, "I promise to be home early tonight, but if you are in trouble - text me. I know I have been very busy, but I'm always here for you. Love, Dad." Around 7:30 p.m. his dad finally arrived home. Johnny instantly ran up to him and gave him a big hug.

"Hi, Son. Where's your mom?"

"There's another emergency at the hospital, and she ran back to work. But Cathy made chicken pot pies and left one in the oven for you."

"Great, I'm starving. Let me go upstairs and change. Then we can sit and talk at the table."

"Ok, Dad."

"Did you finish studying math?"

"Yup, I just finished the last math problem. You know, the video math game you bought me is really helping and is surprisingly making math kind of fun."

"I knew you'd like it, Son."

While Mr. Prospect went upstairs to change, Johnny shut his video game console and set the table for his dad.

"Dad, I'm so excited you are home. You've been working so much and there have been so many things I wanted to talk to you about," Johnny said, calling up the stairs in an eager voice.

"Such as, Johnny?" his dad asked, arriving in the kitchen with a smirk on his face. "Does it have to do with your birthday party plans?"

"Not really. That isn't as important right now. Something strange happened, and I need you to be honest with me."

A look of worry crossed Mr. Prospect's face. Johnny always knew when he was worried because his dad would squint and raise one eyebrow like a triangle.

His father slowly put down his fork, rubbed his chin, and asked Johnny, calmly, "What is it, Son? Are you ok?"

"I think so, Dad. The weirdest thing has happened twice. And I know I'm almost nine and everything, and I know I shouldn't be acting like a kid, but…."

"But what, Johnny?" his father interrupted.

"Well, Dad, are Pimbies real?"

"What makes you ask that?"

"I think I saw one, or I dreamt about it. I'm not sure, but it was a very real feeling dream if it actually was a dream."

"Johnny, this is a difficult thing for me to answer. I know you won't understand what I'm about to say, but the concept of 'real' is, in a way, subjective. What I mean by that is, 'real' is different for different people. There are many things that happen in the world that most people do not see. Our eyes and our brains can only absorb so much information at any one time. So sometimes things pass us by, but our brains remember them, and then we dream about them. That doesn't make it fake, but it's not necessarily what we'd call 'real' like this fork."

Mr. Prospect picked up the fork and banged it on the table for effect. "See, Johnny, you'd say this fork is real, right? But what happened when I banged the fork on the table?"

"It made a loud sound, and you got some pot pie on Mom's curtains."

"Uh-oh, your mom will kill me. We definitely need to clean that up before she gets home, but you're right, the fork made a sound, and that sound was real, right?"

"Sure."

"What about the things you don't see?"

"What do you mean, Dad?"

"Well, sound is a wave, and the waves from the fork are still moving even though we don't hear the sound anymore. So,

31

because we don't notice the waves, does that mean they're no longer real?"

Johnny rubbed his head with both hands. He just didn't get how his dad was answering. He didn't have a clue what his dad meant. Finally, he sighed and said, "You're right, Dad. I've got no clue what you're talking about. The waves still seem real, but I don't get it. And that doesn't tell me if Pimbies are real or not."

Johnny started getting a little upset and impatient, but before he could open his mouth to ask another question, his father spoke.

"Son, I'm trying to explain to you the difference between defining things as real by being able to see them or not. But let me put it another way."

"Yes, please do, Dad."

Mr. Prospect paused to think for a moment before continuing. "Johnny, I truly believe there are many forms of magic and magical beings in the world, as you know. But it's up to you to find out if any of it is real for you. I can't tell you the answer. You have to decide what to believe in for yourself when it comes to this question. The more you grow up, the more you need to make decisions about what to believe in. I know it's difficult at your age, but you also know that I have always liked to challenge you to learn and grow."

"Yeah," Johnny said, interrupting his father. "You used to say you like to stretch my mind," he said laughingly.

"Yes, you need to stretch to grow. Remember how we used to play with globes? Most people don't know where they live, and at five you were learning about different places in the world, right?"

"Right, Dad, I know," Johnny replied all the while thinking to himself, *how strange he's talking about the globes. I just thought about that the other day.* "But I still don't know what you are trying to say."

"All I'm saying is that there are a lot of things people don't notice but they are real; they do exist. People didn't think the atom existed many years ago only to find out that it does. People also thought the earth was flat until they discovered it was round. People thought the earth was the center of the universe until they learned the sun was, in fact, the center. Son, no one can answer the question for you. You're the only one that can ever decide what is real - you have to do the research yourself. Just remember the old saying, there's more than meets the eye."

"I am trying to do research, Dad", Johnny said in a noticeably irritated voice. "I've been searching the Internet, and I haven't found one thing about Pimbies."

"Johnny, I know your generation thinks Google knows everything, but sometimes there are things you can only learn through experience."

"Uffa, Dad, again I have no idea what you mean. But ever since the Pimby appeared, Mickey and I have been acting like Holmes and Watson, yet we haven't found any clues. So I'm not just searching on Google."
"Johnny, let me give you a little piece of advice. You're telling me this Pimby came to you right?"

"Yeah, he even called himself Filbert."

"Well, Johnny, if this thing came to visit you, then my advice is that you have to solve it on your own. It's your mystery. Mickey will have his own mysteries. You just keep your eyes open and see what happens."

"Ah, ok, Dad, but can I ask you something else?"

"Sure, always."

"You're not playing a joke on me, are you? You know, like old times?"

"I wish I had the time to play jokes on you, Son. It'd be fun. I miss those times, Johnny, and I miss being with you very much. But no, I haven't been playing jokes on you."

Right then, Johnny heard that weird humming sound again and looked around the room. He checked if maybe the oven timer was still ticking. Then, he peeked at his video game, thinking it might not have shut down properly.
"Dad, do you hear anything?"

"Like what, Johnny? I hear many things," he said, smirking.

"No, I mean right now, a humming type of sound?"

"Nope. Why? Do you?"

"Yes, in fact, this is the third time I've heard it. It happened the last two times right before the Pimby showed up."

Mr. Prospect didn't respond, but instead just gazed intensely at Johnny. As Johnny looked back at him, he thought he saw a little colorful sparkle in the corner of his dad's left eye. He continued to wait for his dad to say something, but his dad just continued to stare at him with a crooked smile. This was the smile Dad used when he was proud or happy with Johnny. Johnny didn't get why asking about the sound made Dad smile like that. But it had been so long since he saw that smile, he didn't want to spoil it by asking. He just wanted to enjoy the moment.

Finally, his father said jokingly, "Well, Johnny, I guess I should've told you to keep your ears open as well as your eyes when I gave you my advice about your mystery."

"Dad, you really do like to turn everything into a joke!"

"Johnny, of course, why should life be boring? It should be fun, right?"

"I guess. It's just everything has been so bizarre lately."

"Johnny, you are growing up. There will be so many things that happen that will feel abnormal as you grow and change. You're changing, you're growing, and you'll perceive the world differently as you continue to grow. Have fun with the changes, and don't let them worry you so much, ok?"

"Ok, I'll try."

Slowly, just like the other two times, the humming started to fade away, and they spent the rest of the evening talking about all different subjects - exactly what Johnny missed most about having his dad home. They could talk about anything. He always felt like his dad was more of a buddy than just a dad.

"Johnny, why don't we treat ourselves to a piece of Cathy's peach pie?"

"Yum, and ice cream, right?"

"You got it!"

Cathy made great pies, and she'd sometimes give Johnny a piece right out of the oven. For as long as he could remember, Cathy always talked about wanting to write a cookbook. She often used Johnny as a guinea pig, testing many of her recipes on him. He loved it because everything she cooked was incredibly delicious. She used to tell him that cooking was like making a magic potion, which made him even more excited to help her cook when he was younger.

While he gobbled down his second piece of pie, he remembered how he'd continually ask her the same question, "Why is it like making a magic potion?"

She'd always respond in exactly the same way. She explained that people were called witches and wizards a long time ago because they were able to use their imagination to make recipes that people had never thought about. Those people were able to take normal, boring ingredients and create something special by combining them all together in a new way. "That's the power of imagination, Johnny, creating something new, something special."

Johnny stopped in his thoughts for a moment, never realizing how much Cathy talked to him about imagination.

He continued to hear her voice in his head saying "thank you" out loud to the earth, the sun, and the rain for helping all the ingredients grow. Only after saying "thank you" would she then stir everything together.

"Johnny, never forget," she'd tell him repeatedly, "that being thankful for everything we have is a super powerful form of magic."

The picture of Cathy standing over a big mixing bowl popped up so clearly in his mind. He saw her putting both hands over her heart with her eyes closed, then raising them high above the bowl and saying, "And now for the most important ingredient of all - love." After opening her hands, without fail, she'd turn to Johnny and ask if he'd seen the flash of love fall from her hands. He never did but recalled how much fun it was to try and catch sight of it.

When she finally finished cooking, she explained to him that the only way to make sure the spell was cast was for her to take all the joy in her heart for being part of their family and use it as special energy to make a wish that everyone would enjoy what she made. And poof, magic.

Wow, it's been a long time since I sat with Cathy while she was cooking, he thought to himself.

Cathy started working for Mr. and Mrs. Prospect a week after Johnny was born. By now, he thought of her as more of an aunt than a nanny. Cathy was about 50 years old and, for some reason, had never been married nor had any children. She never spoke about her personal life, and Johnny's parents forbid him to ever ask, but he always wondered about it.

Around 9:00 p.m., Mr. Prospect told Johnny he'd better go up to his room because his mom would be home soon, and he hadn't finished the studying his mom asked him to do.

"Johnny, I know you wish you didn't have to study in the summer like the rest of your friends, but your mom worries about you and only wants what's best."

"I know, Dad."

"And Son, there's much more to life than education from books, so keep your mind open and use the things that happen in your life to teach you as well. I believe experience can sometimes be more important than book learning. Everything can add to your growth. Ok?"

Johnny looked at his dad, feeling super confused because Dad kept saying strange stuff. Once more, Johnny didn't understand what Dad was getting at. He had no clue about keeping his mind open. He imagined a door in his head staying open, and that made him giggle.

"Okay, Dad," he said as he headed up the stairs to his room. Then he turned and shouted, "Goodnight!" down the stairs.

Goodnight, son, sogni d'oro," his father replied. Johnny loved it when his dad said that, it means "golden dreams" in Italian.

Boy, he was acting so strangely tonight. I wonder why he kept looking at me with that grin and what he meant about keeping my mind open. And what in the world did he mean about experience? Johnny thought as he headed up the stairs to his room shrugging his shoulders.

His mom had scheduled more math homework than ever before, but he'd fallen behind because of his sleepovers with Mickey. He promised her that he'd finish all the problems by the next morning, but his eyes felt so heavy. In no time, he slumped in his chair and his head bobbed like a chicken.

Ugh, I'm way too tired. I only have nine problems left. I'll do them in the morning before she leaves for work, he thought to himself as he turned on his fan. The heatwave had not yet broken.

As Johnny gazed out the window, he noticed something odd about the burnt branch of the maple tree. It didn't look like a snake anymore. It seemed more like a long arm with an open hand, palm facing up.

That's strange, he thought to himself. *I've looked at that tree almost every day since it was struck by the lightning bolt, thinking it was cursed or something, and now it looks so peaceful. It must be the light from all the stars tonight.*

He turned around and walked over to his bed. As soon as he laid down, he heard the humming again. But this time he smiled to himself. Johnny felt much calmer now that he'd chatted with his father.

"I'm not going to worry about the humming sound. My dad said this was a mystery that I must solve on my own," he said under his breath. As he shut off the light and rolled on his side, making himself comfortable he quietly spoke out loud, "Filbert, I'm waiting." Johnny, in no time, fell fast asleep, picturing the crooked smile on his dad's face.

"Psst…Psst."

Johnny woke up easily, rubbed his eyes, and as expected read 1:08 a.m. on his alarm clock.

As he walked over to the window, he observed a glowing rainbow-type light up in the tree. In fact, peering out from his window, he could clearly see that the creature was sitting exactly in the middle of what only hours before he'd noticed looked like an open hand, palm facing up. The longer he looked at the tree, the more it seemed like that shiny statue his dad got from a trip to Thailand.

Johnny had never seen such a weird kind of light before. It wasn't just colorful, it looked strange, almost like a liquid. Sort of like pen ink, or that jelly stuff, or even the gooey slime he and Mickey played with.

He couldn't stop staring at the light. The more he gazed at it, the more he felt safe and warm, as if he were being hugged. Then, without thinking, he slowly reached out his arm to try and touch the light, forgetting the window screen was closed. Just before putting his arm through the screen, he got pushed back about two feet. In that instant he heard the vibrating voice of Filbert in his mind saying, "Careful, Johnny, I do not want you to get hurt on the day of our first outing."

Johnny shook his head from side to side and wildly searched his mind for a logical reason to explain what had just happened. That is when he heard his father's voice so clearly that he spun around expecting to see him at his bedroom door. Yet the door was still closed.

"Keep your mind open, Son!"

"Keep my mind open," he repeated silently to himself, not truly understanding what it meant. Then he slowly approached the window once more. There sat the Pimby in the palm of the hand of the big maple tree, glowing ever more brightly that soon, Johnny couldn't see anything but the multi-colored light everywhere. In fact, he had to close his eyes from the intensity. Then the strangest thing happened. Johnny found himself sitting with Filbert in the open palm of the burnt branch of the maple tree.

What? This can't be real! I can't be in the tree, thought Johnny. *It's impossible because the branch was always way too small for me to climb on. How can I be in the tree? How did I get here? What's happening?*

So many questions filled Johnny's head all at once, but he couldn't answer any. He felt frozen, but it was weird, he didn't feel scared or in danger.

"I am glad you opened your mind," Filbert said to Johnny before continuing, "Now before you ask your questions Johnny, know you are safe. Know there are things that will happen when we are together that will be difficult for you to understand. That is because we come from different parts of the same world. Though you should be able to feel deep inside you that you are safe and not in any danger."

"I do," Johnny said confidently, realizing he hadn't even moved his lips. He panicked, trying to speak, but no words came out. Then he noticed something strange – Filbert hadn't moved his lips either. Johnny felt nervous and stared at Filbert, looking worried.

Instantly, he heard Filbert's voice again. "I spoke like a human the first time we met because I am bound to follow the rules in your world when I first introduce myself. Only when you know my name can we then communicate the way we do in my world."

Johnny, both amazed and nervous at Filbert's voice echoing in his mind, kept saying to himself "just keep my mind open." Despite being unclear what that phrase genuinely meant, saying it somehow made him feel slightly calmer. He also found himself giggling over the idea of how crazy he must look, speaking to a magical creature on a burnt branch of a maple tree.

Sitting no more than three feet from Filbert, Johnny noticed something weird. Filbert looked kind of see-through, like Johnny could put his hand right through him. He did look a bit like a chipmunk, but the colors shone so brightly that it was hard to see him properly. What was even weirder was the bright light didn't hurt Johnny's eyes anymore. It made him feel relaxed and safe. Inside Filbert, the colors swirled like smoke stuck in a bubble. The bright light surrounded them both.

"Johnny, we Pimbies do not have any real shape. We are sort of balls of light or energy. When it comes time to visit a child, we take the shape of an animal meant to guide the child. In fact, we are called a PIMBY because we are a combination of **P**ossibilities, **I**magination, **M**agic, **B**elieving and **Y**ou. You see Johnny, life is full of possibilities, and we come to show you how life is meant to be lived: through awareness of all the possibilities that exist and then in taking action to live your best life possible."

"Wait, what? How can you be part of me, or me be part of you?" Johnny asked in the most confused voice.

"Johnny, we come from different parts of the same world, as I mentioned to your earlier, but trust me, we are connected in ways you have yet to understand. A lot of what I say may be a bit over your head, but I need you to let go of trying to understand and instead be curious. Can you do that?"

"Ah yeah, kinda confusing. But ok, I can try Filbert, but I really don't understand anything you are talking about. Plus, why would a chipmunk be important to me?"

"Well, Johnny, there will be many things you will not understand at first, but over time you will come to understand everything. You just need to be patient. Think of it as we are planting seeds and you need to wait for them to sprout. As for my animal form, there are many old traditions that explain that each person has a special animal guide for their life. Sometimes people even dream about these animals. Chipmunks are of course cute, but they are also highly intelligent. The ancient people used to say that dreaming about a chipmunk meant that something good was on its way, something that would bring laughter and smiles. Others say the image of a chipmunk means that one is going to have a particularly important conversation with someone and need to pay attention."

"I always liked to watch chipmunks play when I went camping with my dad. Maybe that's the reason?"

At that moment, there was a loud sound as if someone suddenly jammed on the brakes of a speeding car and, poof, Filbert abruptly changed shape into a bear. Johnny became so scared that he wanted to run away, but he didn't know where to go.

"Johnny, would it be better if I were a bear?"

"No Filbert, I don't know why, but I feel more comfortable with you as a chipmunk."

"Well, Johnny, that's your answer. I am meant to be a chipmunk for you." Filbert said before turning back into a chipmunk.

He continued, "For someone else, I will be a bear, which means that they have been sleeping too long in life and I need to wake them up. Others might need me to be a deer, which in ancient times meant a signal for some positive change. Still others will need me to be a hawk, which means they need the courage to see the world differently. Everyone in the world is different, and each person needs their own special guide. Does that make sense?"

"Yes, Filbert, I get it."

"Johnny, I also know you feel like the light is surrounding us."

"Yes, Filbert, I feel like I'm floating inside of it. This is all very bizarre."

"Well, Johnny, you feel as if you are floating in the light because you actually are. I have invited you into the world of the Pimbies and our world is full of light. There is so much I have to explain to you, but before we can go any further, I must ask your permission since that is the way of the Pimbies."

What for?" Johnny asked, sounding a bit unsure.

"Permission to change the way you will see the world. It is scary for many people to change the way they see things. It is every child's right from the moment they are born to have a Pimby visit them right before their ninth birthday. But we cannot force any child to take the journey. Every child has to accept it. It is like I am offering a ticket to go on an adventure."

"What if I say no?"

"Nothing will happen, Johnny. You will wake up and not remember this and life will not change."

"And if I say yes, life will change?"

"Not exactly, Johnny, but you will be given the opportunity to learn new ways to view life, which could change everything if you let it."

"Change things in a good way, Filbert?"

"That is an interesting question, Johnny. It is also a question I cannot answer for you. Only you can, and only at the end of the journey."

"Hmm, Filbert, maybe I needed you to be the hawk so I could have more courage."

"Ha-ha, Johnny, the fact that I am not a hawk means you have all the courage you need. You just have to decide."

Johnny heard his father's voice once again and wondered if he'd known what was going to happen tonight. Keep your mind open son repeated in his mind over and over.

"Filbert, before I decide, can I ask you why Pimbies come during the ninth birthday and not during other birthdays?"

"Great question, Johnny! What number comes after nine?"

"Ten."

"And how many digits are in the number ten, Johnny?"

"Two. Why Filbert?"

"Just to demonstrate something to you, Johnny. Nine is the last single digit of your life. It is a year of great transition. It is a time when you can learn many new things if you let them seep into your brain. The way a sponge absorbs water. And we come to make sure the water is full of nourishment."

"Hmm, ok, Filbert. I guess that sort of makes sense."

"So, Johnny, what about your permission?"

"Yes, Filbert, I give my permission. I want to see things differently!" Johnny said, feeling both really excited and a little nervous.

The colors started to burst like fireworks, and Johnny felt little shocks all over his body, the kind of shocks one gets during a cold winter day when touching a blanket. He didn't have time to ask Filbert another question before hearing Filbert's voice in his head.

"Johnny, in our world we call it 'stretching.' It is not really that you will see things differently as much as stretching your mind to see many more things. You make room for the magic. It's like how people need to stretch to become great athletes, but in this case, we are stretching your brain."

That is the same word my dad used to use, Johnny thought to himself.

He then chuckled, thinking about his brain stretching like Silly Putty. He really liked Silly Putty because his dad played with it a lot. His dad would stretch and pull it when he worked from home. Once, his dad showed him how Silly Putty could grab pictures from old newspapers, like magic! He'd press the putty on a page, say "abracadabra," and show Johnny the picture stuck to the putty. Then he'd roll it back into a ball, telling Johnny that the picture had become a part of the Silly Putty's memory forever.

Johnny, did you know your memory is just like Silly Putty?" his dad asked him.

"Come on Dad, that's just nuts. I don't believe you!"

"Johnny, I'm not joking. Think about it. Every day you see and do so many different things, and they just become part of your memory - many times without you even knowing that you've absorbed the information, just like the Silly Putty."

"Dad, that's plain nonsense. I study and know what I'm learning."

"And things you don't study? Johnny, tell me the name of the business on the corner of Maple and Stone."

"Ah, it's Pete's Pub."

"And how did you know that Johnny? I find it hard to believe you've been studying the map of Hopewell Junction. Have you?"

"No, but, hmm, well the picture of Pete's just popped into my head."

"See, Johnny? Just like the Silly Putty, your brain absorbed pictures of things, and now they're part of your memory."

"That's weird, Dad."

"Lots of things are weird when you first learn about them."

Johnny thought it was really weird how he remembered their whole talk like it just happened yesterday. He then remembered the coolest thing his dad had told him about Silly Putty - that in 1968 the astronauts took Silly Putty into outer space to play with.

Johnny saw that Filbert was also giggling.

"Filbert," Johnny asked, "are you laughing because you know what I'm thinking about?"

"Johnny, let us just say for now that we are connected, but I promise everything will become clearer in time. You have an amazing imagination that will make our time together tons of fun. Imagination is extremely important in life."

Johnny was so electrified about everything happening that he didn't care about the time or how tired he'd be the next day. He didn't even care that most of what Filbert said didn't make any sense to him. He just thought that all of this was so awesome. So awesome that nothing else really mattered. Also, since he'd given Filbert his permission, he continued to feel tingles all over his body, which made everything feel super magical.

He started daydreaming about what types of adventures they would go on together. Would they find buried treasures, see ghosts, sail the oceans? His many questions burst out all at once, "Filbert, where are we going to go? What will we get? How long will we go for?"

"Johnny, there is still much to do before I can explain how everything works, but it is not like you are thinking. They will not be like ordinary types of trips, such as a visit to an amusement park. There will be treasures if you choose to see it that way, but I am sorry to tell you there will be no gold at the end of the rainbow."

Before Johnny could even respond, Filbert continued. "Johnny, I need you to be a little patient and save your questions for later because tonight we have to go on a really important adventure. This is my third visit to you, and the number three is a powerfully magical number. It is only on the third visit that this journey can take place. I know you have a lot of questions, and I have a lot more to explain to you, but we must save that for another night. For now, I need you to close your eyes."

Johnny couldn't believe how he didn't feel the least bit anxious or afraid anymore. In fact, nothing about this felt unusual any longer. It seemed totally natural to be sitting on a burnt limb of a maple tree, talking to a creature made of light, getting ready to go on a magical adventure. He laughed to himself as he closed his eyes and felt a warm, soft, almost fluffy type of wind swirl around him. He had the sensation that he was being packaged in cotton candy.

"Johnny," Filbert started, "tonight our goal is to find your magical home. This is a place of power, safety, rest, and unlimited possibilities for you. It is a place you will always be able to return to in your mind, a place where you can figure out answers to any questions or problems you face in your life. To find it, you have to create it. And I will tell you how."

By this time, Johnny was breathing quite heavily with excitement while trying to keep his eyes shut as tightly as possible. He fought the urge to open them because all he wanted to do was see what was happening around him. He couldn't understand how he was going to create his magical home but had started trusting that Filbert would explain everything.

"Johnny, in the land of Pimbies, we create with our imagination. That is exactly what we are, pure imagination. It is why we are so many colors all at the same time and resemble smoke to you. A big part of who you are is also imagination, but in the human world, people lose touch with that part of themselves as they grow up. People stop playing 'pretend,' they stop daydreaming, and they start focusing more on limitations. Limitations are things that get in the way. You can think of them as obstacles, like if you were in a car and a big boulder rolled down a mountain and blocked the road you were on. These limitations stop people from believing in the magic of life. One of our jobs is to show you that obstacles are there to teach you something, not to block you. Do you know one of the smartest people ever was a man named Albert Einstein?"

"Duh, yeah, Filbert - everyone knows that by my age. My dad talked about him often. In fact, he used to tell me some quote Einstein said about play, but I can't really remember it."

"Could it be this quote, Johnny? 'Play is the highest form of research. In our child's eyes, the playground is more than just metal and plastic pieces. It is where they can turn on their imagination and be whatever they want to be'. Does that sound familiar?"

"Wow, yeah Filbert that is it. My Dad said he really liked Einstein because he thought in a really different way. He even had a picture of him in his office in the city. But I don't know, he looked a little crazy to me. His hair was a mess."

"That is true," Filbert responded, chuckling. "He did indeed look like a crazy professor. But his work literally changed the world, and he is famous for saying, 'Imagination is more important than knowledge. For knowledge is limited to all we now know and understand, while imagination embraces the entire world, and all there ever will be to know and understand.' He believed that everyone should never lose their childlike curiosity. He understood that everything is created in imagination first and then in the real world."

"Wait, Filbert, my mom tells me all the time that I have to stop with childish things and grow up. Does that mean I can tell her that Albert Einstein said that she's wrong, that he thought we should never grow up and always be like children?"

"No, Johnny, what Einstein wanted is that people never lose their ability to view things like a child, with free imagination, thinking of all possibilities and all the different ways to do things. He wanted people to be flexible and free with their mind because only then can people see many solutions and find new ways to build great things or live better lives."
Filbert continued, "Remember, everything that you see around you, a bridge, a phone, a light, music, poetry, even a farm, all came from someone's imagination first. The point is that I need you to use your imagination. On this trip it will be a little different than how you have used it in the past. I need you to use what we call 'pure imagination.' Pure imagination is not specific; it is free flowing. We will start with a few basic building blocks, and out of that we will find your special place."

"Ah, ok, Filbert. I had hoped to tell my mom that it's ok for me to play more with Mickey and not do my math homework," Johnny said, snickering with his eyes still closed.

"But Filbert, what do you mean by specific?" Johnny abruptly asked.

"By specific, Johnny, I mean thinking too much about details. I mean overthinking and getting stuck on one part. That behavior will block you from seeing all the different ways to do something. Instead, imagination works best when it is flexible. What I want is that you let your imagination flow. Feel free to think of anything you want. Nothing is right or wrong. When you are flexible, you are opening a door. When the door is open, possibilities come flowing in like big waves, and those waves are endless. They allow you to create something fantastic. Do not worry Johnny. I will guide you."

Johnny, fighting hard not to open his eyes, listened patiently to what Filbert said, even though he still felt really confused. Yet, in some way, he knew that his understanding would grow as he spent more time with Filbert. That made him feel better, like it was okay not to know everything.

"Let's begin," Filbert announced as if the King and Queen were coming. "I want you to take three deep breaths in through your nose and out through your mouth, and after each breath I want you to say, 'My mind is open to creation and imagination.'"

Johnny did as he was told. After the second breath, he felt as if he were falling backward. Startled, he reached out to grab hold of something to stop his fall, only to hear Filbert say, "Do not be scared, Johnny. You feel like you are falling because you are sinking into the creative world. Just go with it."

After the third breath, Johnny felt as if he were floating, supported by the whirling warm cotton candy-like wind that had been circling him since the moment he closed his eyes. If truth be told, Johnny had the strangest feeling that he was spinning around in the night sky for all the neighbors to see.

"Johnny, are you ready?"

"Yes, Filbert. Can I open my eyes?"

"Not yet, Johnny. I will tell you when. I will begin to ask you a few questions now. First, I want you to tell me that if you had a special place all yours, what color would you want it to be?"

"Gold!" Johnny yelled out, letting his excitement get the best of him. Johnny was surprised at his choice. He had never even thought about liking the color and certainly didn't own anything gold. *Cool,* he thought to himself.

"Ok, together we will now start to build your special place. Remember to do your best to not get stuck in the details. If you find yourself thinking about the details or feel like you are getting stuck, then say out loud, in a big deep voice 'I AM FLEXIBLE' three times. After you do that, you will reopen the door to imagination, and I will be able to go on to the next question."

"But how will I know if I'm getting stuck? I really don't understand what you mean."

"Trust me, Johnny. You will know."

Johnny nodded his head, letting Filbert know he trusted him.

"Next question, Johnny. What does the landscape look like?"

"There are mountains in the distance, and they form a circle around me."

"Wonderful," Filbert said enthusiastically. "Are there any animals?"

"Yeah. There are monkeys, elephants, lots of rabbits and even colorful strange birds."

"Now, it is time for you to focus on constructing the building. You can think of it as your clubhouse or castle. It will be all yours. Tell me, is it big or small?"

"Big."

"How big?"

"Grand!" Once again Johnny stunned himself with his answer. He almost opened his eyes to ask how big grand was, especially because he'd never used the word before. He started to think of all the details he would see on a grand building, such as the number of windows, doors, and the type of roof. As he thought about the details, he felt the warm wind swirling around him start to get cold and feel tight. It started feeling less like cotton candy and more like coarse twine. Somehow, he understood that the change in the wind meant he was getting stuck in the details and thought to himself, *ah, that's what Filbert meant when he said I'd know.* Then recalling Filbert's directions, he swiftly recited, "I AM FLEXIBLE," three times in a deep voice. The wind promptly returned to its comforting warm, fluffy texture.

"Good for you, Johnny, for noticing you were getting stuck and that your imagination was cooling off. You are very observant. That is a marvelous skill to have."

"We are almost there," Filbert continued. "Only a few more questions to go."

Johnny sensed the increasing delight in Filbert's voice. Since they met, Filbert tended to speak in a rather constant low voice, but now Filbert sounded like a kid wanting to open his Christmas presents. Johnny didn't think it could be possible, but even he became more excited about what was happening.

"Johnny, tell me, what does this place smell like?"

Johnny hesitated for a moment, not truly having ever considered the smell of a particular place. He started thinking of many different types of smells, such as his kitchen when Cathy made her pies, or the smell of the forest, or the city, even the smell of his shampoo. While listing all the different smells he could think of, he again noticed the wind slowing down. Now knowing that was a signal his creative process was cooling off, he yelled out, "I AM FLEXIBLE," three times and then answered Filbert, "It smells sweet."

"Johnny, you are very advanced for your age. Many people do not notice the changes in the winds of creation so quickly. I am thrilled to be your Pimby. We are getting closer. I have two more questions. First, what does it sound like?"

"Singing," Johnny answered.
He started to realize that he only had to say what came to his mind from his heart. It was just that simple. He only had to think about what made him feel good inside and give answers that gave him a feeling similar to how he felt when he got to spend time alone with his dad.

"Final question Johnny. What is your one special, favorite thing in this place?"

"A WATERFALL!" Johnny screamed out, feeling as if he'd just scored the winning goal. The waterfall at Crooked Creek Falls happened to be his most favorite thing about moving out of the city. He felt himself smile about how amazingly perfect that answer was because the waterfall was the place where his dad told him the Pimbies played.

He wanted to open his eyes so badly but waited for Filbert to tell him what to do next. Then, he sensed many things beginning to change around him. He heard weird creaking and popping sounds. It also seemed the creative wind came to a complete stop. Next, he felt the temperature start to rise. He also started to smell the fragrance of many different flowers. One scent stood out more than any other. Though he couldn't name it, he knew it was the same smell from the sticks his father burned the night he played the frosted glass bowl.

I wonder why the memory of that bowl keeps coming into my mind? It's so strange. I've never thought about that bowl before.

He then heard water and he knew they'd arrived, but where, he didn't have any clue. He was amazed that he had the strength to keep his eyes closed. He held them shut so tightly that he wondered if he'd be able to open them when the time came. Finally, he heard music. It was a type of music unlike anything he'd ever heard in his life. In a way, it sounded like a choir, but in a language and rhythm, he didn't know.

"Welcome," was all Filbert said before Johnny opened his eyes so widely that he reached up to keep his eyeballs from falling out. There in front of him was the most unbelievable sight he'd ever seen. It felt like minutes before he could blink, fearing that if he did, this amazing place would disappear.

Before him stood a golden temple, twice as tall as a telephone pole, and built in an oval shape. The entire building was made of solid gold and shined so brightly in the sun, yet it didn't bother his eyes to gaze upon it. The way the sun reflected on the building made it seem like the building was pulsing. In a bizarre way, Johnny had the impression that the temple was actually breathing.

The waterfall, in the distance, came down over a stony cliff and drained into a small lake where, shockingly, the temple floated.

The land where both the temple and lake sat was flat, with the most beautiful flowers Johnny had ever seen. They were so fragrant that it reminded him of being in the perfume section of a department store.

On the horizon in all directions were jagged, high mountains, which reminded him of a vacation he and his family had taken to Arizona. The mountains were very rocky, with small trees and cacti, and the most beautiful colored dirt. In fact, the longer he looked around, the more he became aware of all the colors surrounding him: the red earth, the blue sky, the green bushes, the red, orange, pink, violet, and white flowers, and the golden temple.

Then he heard the trumpet of elephants, and in the distance, he saw monkeys, deer, and rabbits. *What a wonderful place*, he thought to himself before turning to Filbert.

"Filbert," Johnny whispered. He couldn't understand why he whispered, but this place made him feel like he should. "Where are we? Is this a real place?"

"Johnny, there are many things you are going to learn while we are together. You will see that the world is much more magical than most people know. You will discover that you can create things with your thoughts if your heart is in the right place. This place is real to you. It is, in reality, part of you. In fact, if you look closely, you will notice that your temple seems to be breathing, just as you are breathing. If you are asking if you can find it on a map or travel here by plane, well that is something that is too early to answer. For now, accept that you found this place because you did not limit yourself. You let yourself be free with your thoughts. You were flexible and that is when your words and thoughts can create magic. The Pyramids are a real place today, but they started in someone's mind, heart, and imagination. That person used to visit them over and over again in their imagination. Now they are a real place on the earth. In fact, as I said earlier, everything around you, everything built by people, first started in someone's imagination. They were so real to the people who imagined them, that they were able to create them on the earth."

Filbert went on to explain that every single person has a special place in their heart where they can connect to the magic of life. All they have to do is believe it is there. And if they open their minds and hearts, they will find it.

"Johnny, may I tell you a secret?" Filbert asked with a whimsical tone to his voice.

"Of course Filbert," Johnny responded with great enthusiasm.

"There is not one temple exactly like this in the entire universe because you are unique. It is an expression of your uniqueness. No one can ever be you as you can never be anyone else. You will learn during our time together that magic is powered by many forces and your uniqueness is a great source of your magic. No one can ever add the same value to the universe as you do."

Just then, the music started to grow louder. Johnny glanced around but couldn't figure out where it was coming from, especially as he didn't see any other people.

"Filbert," Johnny asked, "what's making the music I'm hearing? Are there other people here?"

"Johnny, this is a place created from your imagination, which is a type of magic, and all magic has a special sound. When I asked you those questions you created this music with your answers. Again, this music is unlike any other music because you are unlike any other person. This music is unique to you and your heart. Technically the music is made from the magical wind blowing through the trees. As for your other question, Johnny, this is your place, and only you and I are here."

"Cool!" Johnny yelled. "I love the sound of the music, but it seems to be another language and I can't understand what it means."

"In time you will understand everything about this place because it is part of you. You may think you know a lot about yourself already, but as people grow, they learn more about themselves if they want to. In ancient Greece there was a very intelligent man, a philosopher named Socrates who said, 'Know thyself.' He believed that was the reason for life. We Pimbies believe the same thing. In fact, part of everyone's journey on earth is to understand the special parts about themselves. This place represents a big, wonderful part of yourself. You are here to grow and learn and as you do you will uncover more and more magic in this place. In turn, you will learn its language. Johnny, why don't you take some time and walk around for a bit? Get familiar with your special place. I will wait for you next to the waterfall."

Johnny slowly walked over to the golden temple, still unsure of its existence. He slowly walked up the nine steps and stopped in front of the entrance. He counted 27 gold pillars. Each was covered with 27 carvings of flowers, birds, monkeys, and even elephants etched into the gold. He knew he could spend hours examining each one. They resembled pillars his father had told him about years ago in Rome, Italy.

Just then, he heard his father's voice carried by the wind blowing through the temple, "Son, this is called Trajan's Column. It's found in the center of Rome, near what used to be called the Fori Imperiali, which was the center of the Ancient Roman Empire. The Romans used stone columns as storybooks. They would carve important historical events into the stone so the people could remember significant events and learn from them."

This place is totally amazing, Johnny thought to himself.

The floor was made from a black stone he'd never seen before. It reflected the gold like a mirror, giving the impression that he was walking on a tiger skin carpet. Most of the temple didn't have any walls, just pillars that opened to the outside air. In the center of the temple were two huge gold doors that led to a square-shaped room. Golden statues of animals lined the walkway leading up to the doors. As he approached the doors, he felt an extremely strong vibration coming from inside the room. He started to think about when his dad banged the fork on the table the other night and asked him if the sound waves were real.

I'm sure he was setting me up to understand some of this. He must know what's going on.

Johnny reached out his hand to touch the doors when he sensed the vibration suddenly weaken. At the same time, he was overcome by a strange feeling in the center of his chest. He didn't know why but understood it wasn't the right time to open the doors. So, he backed away and walked down the steps.

Johnny was filled with incredible joy that he could call this place "his place." He sat in the grass cross-legged and gazed at the temple, his temple.

A few minutes passed, and Johnny felt the warm wind slowly start twirling around him. He realized it was telling him it was time to head back home. He had no idea how long he'd been away or even what day it was, but he didn't care. He knew his father would understand. He couldn't wait to share this adventure with him. He stood up and walked over to Filbert who was floating above the waterfall.

"Johnny, before we go, there are two things I must explain to you, well, honestly, three," Filbert said correcting himself. "The first is you are not to share any of our travels until your birthday. I know it seems unfair especially because I can tell you are very excited. However, this is a journey for you and you alone and you must complete it before sharing it. It is like pouring all the ingredients of a birthday cake on a table, sticking a candle in it, and singing 'happy birthday' without baking the cake first. There is no cake if you do not bake it, right? Can you understand?"

"I guess so," Johnny replied. "It's just that my dad knows about Pimbies. He used to tell me so many stories about them, and I think he'd stay home more at night instead of working so we could talk about you."
"I understand, Johnny, but it has to be this way for me to continue to visit with you. These are the rules of the journey."

"Ok," Johnny said in a disappointed tone. He then asked, "Filbert, what would happen if I said something by accident?"

"Johnny, do your best to keep it to yourself. Just know that it could end our journey together and you will forget our trips and that you even met me."

"Filbert, that is so harsh and sad."

"Johnny, you will understand that staying committed and honoring your promises are very important to your connection to imagination. Just trust me, ok?"

"Ok" Johnny said in an even more disappointed voice.

"Secondly, Johnny, you do not ever have to worry about time when we are together. You will return exactly at the same time I came to visit you. No time will ever be lost. In fact, one of the secrets you will learn is that time can never be lost. It can be abused, wasted, or spent, but never lost, which is why you need to spend it wisely. But that is getting ahead of ourselves."

Filbert then became flat like a wall clock, his two hands pointed at one and eight, and he said, "For now, just realize it is still 1:08 a.m. in your world."

"Excellent", Johnny said, laughing at Filbert before he puffed back into his chipmunk shape.

"Filbert, will I feel tired?" Johnny asked.

"Not at all. In fact, you will have a great night's sleep and have more energy than you have ever had because you are starting to connect to the unlimited source of all energy in the world - IMAGINATION."

"Awesome!"

"Lastly, we Pimbies only have the ability to visit with humans right before their ninth birthday and only several times during the nine weeks before. Your ninth birthday is the moment when all magic comes together. Three and nine are extremely powerful numbers in our world, which is why it is only on the third visit that we can take this special journey. Children are the most receptive to our teachings right before their ninth birthday. That is why, since the beginning of time, we come only during this period in your life. It is the best moment for us to connect with our seedlings. We can never visit ever again after the age of nine."

"What?" Johnny responded. "I'll never see you again after my ninth birthday? That's so sad! And what the heck is a seedling?"

"A seedling is what we call the children we visit in order to show them a bigger world than they knew existed. We think of it as replanting them in a larger pot, so we call them seedlings. As for your other question about seeing each other in the future, I will answer that in time. Ok?"

"Ok. The seedling thing is strange, but ok," was all Johnny could say before feeling the warm, soft wind pick up speed. He then noticed all the colors of the rainbow wrap around them like a big cyclone. Johnny hadn't seen the colors the last time because he had his eyes closed.

"From now on Johnny, you can keep your eyes open."

"Cool," Johnny replied excitedly.

As he looked more closely, he found that the colors formed a tunnel that they were speeding through. He watched the colors race by, feeling like he was in some crazy amusement park ride. He didn't know if he could talk with Filbert during the journey because of the whistle of the swooshing colors flying by. But then he laughed thinking about "talking," because it was really more like telepathy. He and Filbert were really thinking to each other.

"How do I get back to the golden temple?" he asked.

"The same way you did when we started, Johnny," Filbert responded. "Just take three deep breaths, picture the place in your mind, and then say, 'I RETURN.' After a while, you will only have to picture it in your mind, and you will no longer have to say the words."

Johnny sensed the wind and colors slowing down. He knew they were almost back at his house. He already felt homesick for the beautiful land he'd just visited, yet it was calming to know he could return whenever he wanted.

"Filbert, when will you be back?" Johnny asked, panicking.

"Johnny, when I sense you are ready for my next visit. If you want, I will send you a signal instead of it being a surprise. I will grant you that choice," Filbert said in a very caring voice.

"Filbert, I would like a signal."

"Ok, Johnny. Use your imagination to picture a feather in your mind and let me know when you can see it."

"Got it, Filbert."

"Great, Johnny. The day before my visit I will send you the feather."

"But Filbert, I didn't tell you what kind of feather."

"Johnny, because it is a signal you need me to send you, you have already shared it with me without knowing it. You've invited me into your imagination and shared the picture of the feather with me. It is the same as my traveling with you to your temple or when you thought about the Silly Putty."

"So, you can see all my thoughts?"

"Only those that we share, and only those that you need me to know. Do not worry about me poking around in your head. I am not a mind reader."

Then without warning, Johnny heard a loud popping sound and found himself back in his bed. He jumped out from under the covers and ran to the window to search for Filbert, but he was gone. Johnny turned around and saw that the clock glowed 1:08 a.m.

Could this have all been a dream? It's so strange that he didn't say goodbye, Johnny thought. Then he heard Filbert's voice in his mind, "Why would I say goodbye, Johnny? Goodbye in my world means we would never see each other again. But I will always be with you now. We are connected. Pimbies do not say anything we do not mean because words have magical power. We will talk more about this another time. For now, remember that words are more powerful than you can imagine. Only ever say what is in your heart and never say bad things or gossip about other people because it affects you and the world around you."

"Ah, ok, Filbert, then goodnight."
"Good night indeed" Filbert's voice echoed in Johnny's mind as he climbed back into bed and fell into a deep sleep.

The Tree Exercise

Johnny was sitting on his back porch watching the birds fly around the bird feeder. He couldn't wait for Filbert to visit at 1:08 a.m. and thinking about it made the whole day go really slowly.

Since traveling with Filbert to his golden temple he'd hunted for his special feather every day. As each day went by, he felt more and more let down. He started to think maybe Filbert had totally forgotten about him.

Yet, after he'd woken up and opened his window this morning, a beautiful orange feather with green zebra stripes had floated into his room and landed exactly in the center of his bed. He'd almost jumped through the roof. His immediate reaction had been to run downstairs, find his parents, and show them the strange feather. Then he remembered the "rules" Filbert had given him the last time they were together and had stopped himself. *Dang rules,* he thought.

He'd intended on putting the feather in his memory box, but the instant he dove onto his bed and grabbed it, poof - the feather vanished.

"Of course, I should have known," he said to himself.

Right after Filbert's last visit, things got really strange for Johnny. He tried his hardest to act normal around his family and Mickey, but he felt like they could tell something weird was going on.

The morning following the journey to his temple, Johnny had woken up early and run downstairs to eat breakfast with his dad. He'd wanted to see if his dad would ask him any Pimby questions.

67

Unfortunately, he didn't know that his dad was working at the Summerset Ridge office that morning. That always meant he left incredibly early to get to work on time. Later that day, his mom told him that his father had to stay in Summerset for at least three days. Johnny was amazed that, instead of feeling sad, he didn't mind his father being away. He knew it would make things easier because it would be next to impossible to keep the story of Filbert bottled up from his dad.

Mickey, on the other hand, had completely forgotten about the Pimby story after their sleepovers, when they'd tried to find Filbert a little over two weeks ago. While they did hang out to play, Johnny remained somewhat distant. He wished he had a dollar for every time Mickey asked him, "Dude, you seem spaced out. What's up?"

Even if he could tell others about his trip with Filbert, how would he even start? He could hardly believe it himself, and he was the one who went! It felt strange; he started feeling really alone in the world.

Every night, he'd practiced his breathing just like Filbert taught him, going back to the golden temple again and again. It felt more and more like his own special place every time he visited. He explored the whole temple grounds, watching how the temple shimmered in the water, making it look like there were lots of temples hiding underwater.

He even shared his bananas with the monkeys and rode the elephants! But asking the temple questions, like Filbert said he could, was just too strange for him. He also didn't get how the temple could recharge his batteries or give answers. The more he thought about it, the more confused he got. Some of the things Filbert said were just way too puzzling.

Maybe I should bring my math homework with me next time, he thought, which made him laugh out loud.

Johnny could sense a change happening within him but couldn't exactly describe it. He knew he'd become much more aware of many things around him, such as how all the homes on Wishing Well Lane had slightly different colored lawns and that even though they all had maple trees, each tree had a unique size and shape. He had also observed how the sunlight caused the houses to look unalike from one another depending on the time of day despite they were all painted the same color. Some homes even had more squirrels than others, and certain birds stayed on only one side of the street.

Nearly an hour had passed since Johnny started watching a variety of birds -- finches, robins, cardinals, and doves -- take their turn eating. Some ate directly from the feeder while others waited for seeds to fall to the ground. Others dug through the food looking for certain seeds. What he found even more interesting was how the squirrels waited elsewhere in the yard for the feasting to end so they could eat the remains of what was left on the ground.

I wonder why I never noticed all these little things before, he thought. Another question quickly popped into his head, one that surprised even him, *I wonder why I'm noticing all these things now?*

"Johnny! Dinner!" Cathy called to him from the kitchen window that faced out onto the back porch.

Johnny walked in the back door, took off his shoes, and headed to the bathroom to wash his hands. As he walked into the bathroom, he heard the humming sound. Instead of getting worried as he had the last few times, this time his heart leapt for joy. Now, he felt certain that Filbert was on his way.

69

After walking out of the bathroom, he heard his mom's car pull up in the driveway. She hadn't been home for dinner in quite a while, and it caught Johnny off guard that she was home so early. Still, he was delighted not to be eating alone. Cathy tended to eat with him if his parents weren't home for dinner. He did love Cathy as if she were his aunt, but it wasn't the same as having his parents.

"Hi Mom," Johnny cheerfully yelled from the kitchen.

"Hi, Johnny, how was your day?"

"Fine, thanks. I finished all the math problems you left for me and even beat Mickey at my video racing game three times!"

"Well, it sounds like you had a productive day, Johnny. I'll review the written problems later. But tell me, how did you do on the video math problems?"

"Really well. 98%."

"You have improved so much in the last week Johnny. I'm so proud of you. Keep up the good work."

"I know. For some reason, I'm finally beginning to understand math. I even like the math video game more now. It's like something just clicked and for some reason I feel that learning math is just like learning another language."

"Johnny, that's a great way to think about it. In fact, math really is a type of common language because no matter what languages people speak, math is the only one that is the same for everybody. Two plus two will always equal four in any language," said Mrs. Prospect with a slight grin on her face. "Math is very useful, and you will be glad when school starts that you already understand a lot more of it."

While Cathy served the food, Johnny started to hear the humming sound again, but this time other things began to happen. He shook his head from side to side because he couldn't believe what he was witnessing. He glanced over at his mom and then at Cathy to see if they were aware of anything. But they were talking to each other and acted as if everything was normal. Johnny continued to stare at his plate and then heard Filbert's voice, "Keep your mind open."

With that reminder, Johnny took three deep breaths and just watched as things changed. The food on his plate started to change from cooked to raw. Then it all separated into individual ingredients. Johnny started laughing, as right in front of his eyes, a chicken started clucking, a cauliflower and herbs took root on the table, and a field of wheat sprouted to cover the entire kitchen floor. Then people appeared out of thin air and started to pick the vegetables and took the chicken away. Afterwards, delivery trucks pulled into the kitchen. He turned again to Cathy and his mom to check their reactions, but they continued talking, completely unaware of all the craziness overtaking the kitchen. Johnny watched the workers pack up the trucks with boxes and then with a big "toot, toot" they pulled out of his house.

Following a big flash, the kitchen then transformed to the inside of the supermarket he and Cathy had gone to earlier that day for groceries. As abruptly as it had started, the humming suddenly stopped, and Johnny's food appeared back on his plate.

"Johnny aren't you hungry?" his mom asked.

"Do you not like the meal?" Cathy followed.

"Oh, no, it's great. I was, um, I was just thinking about how hard it is to get all this food."

"What do you mean, Johnny?" Cathy asked. "We just had to walk down to the supermarket in town."

"No, I mean, I've never thought about how much work happens before we are able to buy it. I don't know, I always thought it was just always there in the store. I never really thought about where it comes from or how many people have to work so hard to get it to us."

"What a great thought, Johnny," said Cathy. She then stared him straight in the eye and said, "It is as if we had a whole group of workers in our kitchen."

Johnny gazed at Cathy, shocked. Had she actually seen the people in the kitchen too? He was on the verge of asking her until he heard Filbert whisper "the rules."

Yeah, this is my journey, and I can't let the cat out of the bag. Cathy, still smiling at him in a curious way, continued, telling a story of how her grandmother used to tell her that food has special magic. "My granny used to tell me that everything comes from the stars. So when we eat food, we are really eating stardust."

Johnny noticed that when Cathy talked about her grandmother, she seemed to become a little girl again, which made Johnny smile. Yet, this time as Johnny smiled, he felt something peculiar in the middle of his chest, like an itch, which quickly went away.

"It makes you want to say 'thank you,'" Mrs. Prospect remarked. "There are so many things we have in our lives from people who work extremely hard for us. People we'll never meet. People we'll never be able to say thank you to. Just think about that when you hear a siren, Johnny. That means there are a lot of people working to help someone in need. Isn't that amazing?

That's why we should always say thank you for the things we have."

Johnny felt unusually happy that his mom was paying attention. He was also stunned that his mom was talking like this because she rarely discussed anything, except chores. A big smile came to Johnny's face. Again, he felt a tickle in his chest that passed as quickly as it came.

That is so strange, I hope I'm not getting sick, he thought to himself, a little afraid that being sick would stop him from seeing Filbert.

"Johnny," Mrs. Prospect continued, "you're growing into a fine young man." Then she winked, which was very unusual for her.

Johnny noticed that in the last few days, his mom seemed less stressed, even though she worked a lot, and his dad wasn't home much. He wasn't sure why, but felt it had something to do with Filbert coming into his life. In fact, ever since Filbert had, he'd started witnessing rainbow-colored shimmers of light in many parts of his house every now and again. It seemed as if the light from Filbert remained even though Filbert went back to his world.

The remainder of dinner was boring. Johnny grudgingly finished his cauliflower. It had never been his favorite vegetable. Yet after watching the magical scenes of how it had reached his plate, he felt it was much better not to waste any food. He suddenly had the urge to avoid wasting everything the earth worked so hard to produce. He'd never thought of himself as wasteful but was certainly guilty of always putting too much on his plate and then throwing the remainder down the garbage disposal.

It had never crossed his mind before because everyone he knew acted the same way. He quickly figured out that neither of his parents nor Cathy wasted any food. He thought about how many times they'd tell him his eyes were bigger than his stomach, or how there were people starving all around the world, but hadn't really taken any of it seriously. He now began to understand what it meant to pay attention to his actions.

Following dinner, Johnny went to his room and watched television. He was so restless about Filbert's expected visit that he had a hard time paying attention to anything and constantly flipped channels. He slowly started falling into a daydream about what he and Filbert would do and where they'd travel.

He began picturing taking a magic carpet ride over the city when Filbert's voice whispered in his head, almost sounding like a wind chime, "Keep your mind open Johnny, be flexible. Expectations limit you and set you up for disappointment. When you have expectations, it is like you are trying to predict the future. It is like when people hope it will be sunny, and then it rains. They become unhappy because their expectation was not met. You have to be flexible, Johnny."

So, I need to be flexible. Ok, I can do that. But I have no clue what that crazy chipmunk means by expectations, he thought to himself, returning to flip the channels. Abruptly the remote stopped working.

Johnny was about to go find a new battery when he recalled something curious his dad had told him the last time the remote stopped working. It was something he really hadn't paid much attention to at the time, but for some reason came rushing back into his head now.

"Son, maybe it stopped on this channel because there's going to be something important for you to see. Sometimes the universe does things like that for all of us."

At the time, Johnny had just grabbed the remote from his dad because he didn't want to miss the end of his superhero show. Now he wondered, *if his dad was right about Pimbies, maybe he was right about the TV as well.*

He sat patiently through a few stupid commercials about hair dye, shaving cream, and deodorant. Finally, a game show restarted after a totally girly commercial about nail polish. "Uffa," he said, "enough is enough," finally standing up to get a battery. Just then the host said, "Show Johnny what he has won." Johnny's mouth dropped open. *What a coincidence! I can't believe the guy on TV is named Johnny.*

His eyes were now glued to the TV. He was so into it, wanting to know what happened next. The camera showed a guy, maybe around twenty-one, looking really excited, like he was holding his breath, waiting for something to happen. Next, the camera turned to a polka-dotted curtain. It opened to reveal a brand-new red convertible car. The audience cheered and clapped. The camera quickly returned to the young man whose smile had turned into a frown.

The host then asked, "Johnny, why aren't you excited about your new car?"

"Well," he replied, "I'm a little sad, disappointed really, because I had hoped it'd be blue."

Johnny laughed so hard he slipped off his bean bag chair. He couldn't believe what had just happened. There on the television was an example of someone winning a great prize but because he expected a different color, he felt sad. Johnny understood that it was the guy's expectations that made him sad, when instead, he should've been super happy about winning a new car. In those three minutes, Filbert's comments about expectations clicked for Johnny.

Cool, he thought.

The clock read 9:45 p.m. Johnny knew his mom would be up in a few minutes to tell him it was almost bedtime. He had no idea how he would be able to fall asleep knowing that in only a few hours he would meet with Filbert again. Mrs. Prospect, like clockwork, was right on time with her knock on his bedroom door.

"Johnny, it's almost bedtime. Make sure you brush your teeth and leave your math problems on the hall table before going to bed. Ok?"

"Ok, Mom," Johnny yelled through the door, changing into his pajamas before going into his bathroom to brush his teeth.

After brushing his teeth, he grabbed his homework from his desk that he had finished earlier. As he gazed down at the answers to his math exercises, it dawned on him that the numbers followed a pattern. He was looking at the nine times table: 108, 99, 90, 81, 72, 63, 54, 45, 36, 27, 18, and 9. *All multiples of three and nine, those powerfully magical numbers Filbert told me about. This is way too much of a coincidence.*

He continued staring down at the paper after leaving his room, not paying attention to where he was walking.

"OUCH!" Johnny yelled as he walked right into the hall table and stubbed his toe.

"What happened, Johnny?" His mom said as she ran out of her room.

"Oh nothing, I was just reviewing my answers and not paying attention to where I was walking and stubbed my toe."

"Maybe you should put some ice on it."

"Nah, it will be ok. It was the shock more than the pain that made me yell."

"Alright then, but if it continues to hurt, go downstairs, and get some ice. Promise me you will, ok?"

"Ok, Mom."

Remembering how he'd stubbed his toe last time because of his skateboard, he lightheartedly mumbled, "Filbert, I hope I don't have to stub my toe each time you visit." He continued giggling as he limped back into his room.

He couldn't sleep, so he played his video games quietly with the TV on mute and the lights off so his mom wouldn't know. But lately, playing video games didn't excite him like before. He started feeling being indoors too much was making his world seem very small. Checking his clock, he saw it was past midnight. Turning off the game, he lay in bed, letting his mind wander. He started thinking about all the camping trips he had with his dad when they first moved to Hopewell Junction.

"Being in nature is one of the best things you can do for yourself, Johnny," his father would say as they walked through the trails of the state park searching for a good camping site.

"Why is that Dad?"

"Son, we can all learn many things from nature if we just pay attention. Many of the most powerful people and philosophers spent as much time as they could in nature."

"Really, like who?"

"Remember when we talked about the emperors of Rome? Who was your favorite?"

"Marcus Aurelius."

"Johnny, he used to say we could learn from nature and liked to go to the countryside outside of Rome to think about things. Of course, you remember the story of Sir Isaac Newton and the apple, right?"

"Of course, Dad."

"Want to know something else about how incredible nature can be, Johnny?"

"Definitely!"

"Get this. Bicycle helmets are designed like the skull of a woodpecker."

"Really?"

"Yes, people understood a woodpecker bangs its head all day long trying to get the bugs out of the old trees. One day someone thought about how their skulls must be made in such a strong way that it would be worth researching their skulls to find out how to protect people who might bang their heads."

"Awesome!"

"Johnny, there may come a day when you lose touch with nature and wanting to be outside. I'm hoping that our trips will leave a memory inside you that remind you about how important and fun it is to be outside. We aren't made to be indoors all the time. We need sunlight and fresh air. We all need that type of energy, just like every other living thing on our planet. That is why it is important to care for the earth and avoid pollution, waste, and damaging this amazing planet."

Johnny opened his eyes from his daydream and realized how his father had been spot on. This summer, Johnny had indeed been spending more and more time indoors than ever. He started thinking about how many times this summer he and Mickey fought because Mickey wanted to play outside, which Johnny found boring, opting to play video games instead.

He'd lost touch with nature just like his father warned him. Right at that moment the humming sound started. It was 1:08 a.m. Filbert was right on time. Johnny's heart started to race, and he ran to the window waiting for Filbert to appear on the open palm of the maple tree, only he didn't. Johnny put his hands around the sides of his face and pressed it against the window screen, staring really hard at the tree. Still no Filbert. The humming got louder and louder, and Johnny felt the familiar warm wind start swirling around him. Right away, he closed his eyes and took deep breaths in through his nose and out through his mouth.

The twirling of the wind increased and then Johnny heard Filbert say, "You can open your eyes now, Johnny."

As Johnny did so, he found himself in a completely white place. Nothing at all but white. He felt as if he'd been beamed up into the middle of a thick bright white fog, which looked like the inside of a shinny white eggshell. He turned around in a circle, not sure exactly what he was searching for, perhaps for something other than white. Even Filbert glowed like snow. He had lost all of his rainbow colors and was floating around the egg-shaped room like a cloud.

"Where are we?" Johnny asked.

"We are in the middle of imagination itself. I know this is hard for you to understand but think of this as a type of airport terminal. From here we can voyage to different experiences."

"I'm not sure I understand, Filbert. What happened to your colors? Why didn't I see this place the last time I saw you? Why didn't we start from here before going to the golden temple?"

"Good questions, Johnny. Let me see if I can help you understand. First, the reason you did not see this place during our last trip was because you created the trip from your mind. To get to the temple we started from your imagination. This place is all imagination - all the imagination that has ever been or will ever exist. It is the imagination of the universe. Try and think of it like a bucket, which is basically what it is - more or less. Think of everyone in the entire universe, and pretend they are all imagining at the same time and pouring their imagination into one bucket. Well, this place is the bucket where all the imagination in the universe gets mixed together. When all different colors of light are mixed together, the light becomes white. Do you remember your science class when you learned about sunlight and used the prism?"

"Yeah, sort of. I remember that a prism is a piece of glass shaped like a triangle and learning some strange name for all the colors of sunlight."

"ROY G BIV?" Filbert asked.

"Yeah, ROY G BIV - Red, Orange, Yellow, Green, Blue, Indigo and Violet. I'd forgotten, but I still don't get it, Filbert."

"Johnny, what happens when the sun shines through the prism?"

"You see a rainbow."

"Well, what a prism does is it takes white light and breaks it into all its different colors. You only see a rainbow in the sky when the sunlight shines through water droplets. That is because the drops of water act like tiny prisms. All those different colors you mentioned make 'white light.' White includes all colors, and every person that exists has a favorite color. Don't you?"

"Yes, orange."

"Well, Johnny, what people do not realize is that their favorite color, in reality, is the color of their imagination."

"Wow!"

"Think about the prism again and how the colors are on one side and the 'white light' is on the other side. What do you think would happen if everyone dumped their colorful imaginations into a bucket?"

"It would turn into the color white. I get it!"

"And that is why when I appear to you in your world, I am full of color. It is because I am a piece, or some say 'a figment' of imagination - but not only of yours. Many people have me as their guide. And each person imagines in a different color. So, in your world I always seem like I am changing colors. But here, here in the center of imagination - which may be an easier way for you to think about it - I become white. Does that make sense?"

"Surprisingly, it does, Filbert. Thanks."

"Good. There are a few more things I want to explain to you before we start on our journey tonight. Ok?"

"Of course, Filbert."

"Perfect. First, I know you find my voice sounds like something you heard your father use a few years ago. Right?"

"Yeah, a white bowl. Honestly, it looked like ice. Why?"

"Many, many years ago, Johnny, the world was very, very different. People were much more connected to their imaginations. In the past we did not have to guide people like we have to today. They practiced using their imagination every day and rarely lost touch with it. They believed in magic and miracles. They used different tools to connect to the power of their imagination, to the power of their creativity, which today you call 'inspiration.' In fact, Johnny, the word 'inspiration' comes from two old words that mean SPIRIT WITHIN. So, you can think of 'inspiration' as the magic within you."

"That's so cool! But what does that have to do with the white bowl?"

"Well, about the white bowl. Ancient tribes, long ago, in Northern India used what they called a 'singing crystal bowl.' The sound, which is really just a vibration, helped unlock the creative forces within each person. My voice reminds you of that bowl because I am here to guide you. I am here to connect you to your imagination, to your creative power and to possibilities. But just like everyone has a favorite color, people also have different sounds that are important to them. It has to do with their own vibration. If I were to guide someone else, my voice would sound completely different. Yet, it sounds like the bowl to you because the bowl left its mark inside you. Its vibrations touched you and became part of you."

"That is wild! But Filbert, how could the vibrations from the bowl be part of me? And listen, I do trust you, but seriously…people vibrate?"

"Johnny, you ask wonderful questions for a boy your age. If you stay connected to your imagination, you will understand more as you get older. Let me try and explain everything better. Have you learned that most of your body is made of water?"

"Yeah, my dad told me, but he said I'll learn more about it in biology class when I'm older."

"Well, even though you can't see it, sound is like a wave and those waves are called vibrations."

Johnny quickly spoke with pride in his voice. "I know. My dad actually told me about that. He banged a fork on the table and asked me if the sound waves were real even though I couldn't see them. He actually did that the night I asked him if Pimbies were real."

"Great. He is a good teacher, Johnny. The best way for me to explain what I mean about the sound being part of you is for you to think about it as leaving a song inside you. When the vibration from the bowl touched the water inside you, it caused the water to vibrate. And that caused some of the song to be left inside your body. Think of it as if it were like a drop of green food coloring falling into a big pool of water. While you would not see the water change color, the food coloring is in the water, right?"

83

"I guess," Johnny replied, a little unsure.

"That is what I meant about the vibration of the bowl being part of you. Hmm, I can feel your mind stretching out to me for a better explanation."

"It is? For me, my brain feels stretched to the limit," Johnny said, pulling his ears in opposite directions causing them both to laugh very loudly.

"Johnny," Filbert started, still half giggling. "Have you ever heard the name Masaru Emoto?"

"Who? Is he a Kung Fu master or something cool like that?" Johnny asked with excitement in his voice.

"No, Johnny," Filbert responded with a big smile on his chubby face, amused at the playfulness of Johnny's imagination. "Though some people might find him as interesting as a Kung Fu Master, he was a Japanese businessman who later became a special type of doctor. His job is not important, but what he studied was super interesting. He experimented with water and vibration. I am sure you can read about him on the Internet, but do you want to know what he discovered?"

"Sure, Filbert, but sometimes you make my head spin. Just saying." Johnny said, snickering.

Filbert then raised his head so high in the air that his neck became as thin as a pencil.

"Like this, Johnny?" Filbert asked as his head started to spin like a dreidel on Hanukkah.

Johnny fell to his knees, grabbing his stomach from laughing so hard. "Filbert, you're hysterical." Johnny howled with laughter.

"Learning should always be fun Johnny. Now back to Mr. Emoto. His experiments involved taking normal glasses of water and playing music while he was freezing the water. After the water froze, he examined the frozen crystals under a microscope. He found that soft calm music produced beautifully shaped crystals, while loud harsh music produced ugly crystals. For him it proved that vibration affect water."

"Wicked. Will I learn about that in school, too? It'd be so cool if I already knew the answer."

"I don't think so, Johnny. His work is still not part of most science classes. I just wanted to use it as an example so you could picture the effects of vibration. You can also find his ice pictures on Google if you want. Anyway, did that help you understand the concept better?"

"It did. Thanks Filbert. But I will say that sometimes you use words a bit tough for me:"

"You mean, they are stretching you," Filbert said with a grin.

"Ha-ha Filbert but wait. What about people vibrating? I'm not shaking all over the place right now. I'm not vibrating."

"That is one-hundred percent false, Johnny. That is why we tell our seedlings to 'keep their minds open.' You will learn a lot in school about the things I am telling you, but you will not learn about the magic in them. Anyway, right now, in this moment, I can assure you that you are vibrating. Everything on earth vibrates Johnny because everything on earth is made of molecules. Do you know what they are?"

"Sort of, Filbert, I remember seeing them on a cartoon called Pinky and the Brain. It was one of my favorite shows."

"I know the show," Filbert responded. "Brain always wanted to take over the world if I remember correctly. Well, molecules are constantly moving. I know you think your body is solid, but if you put your hand under a special microscope, you will see it vibrating because the molecules are always in motion. Interesting, right?"

"Yeah, totally and totally puzzling but, yeah, interesting."

"The second thing I wanted to explain is that our journeys, from now on, will be different from the first one. We will always start from this place, and the journeys will be more about seeing things differently and learning. But I promise they will be amazing."

"You're not going to test me, are you?"

"Oh, Johnny, that is really a funny question. I will tell you the answer, but you must realize it is one of the things that I am not allowed to explain to you. Do you still want to ask that question?"

"Yes, are you going to test me?", Johnny exclaimed, sounding a bit forceful.

"No Johnny, I will not test you. Your life from the age of nine onwards will be your test, an ongoing test."

"WHAT?" Johnny yelled so loudly. "An ongoing test - that is crazy!"

"Johnny, please remember to be flexible. The word 'test' has a different meaning in my world than you are used to. Just trust me. That is all I can say."

Johnny sat quietly for a few moments. He started feeling a little stressed and slowly started to think that all of this wasn't as much fun as he had hoped. He closed his eyes and thought to himself, *Should I forget about all of this? Maybe I'm in over my head.*

POP! Johnny quickly opened his eyes and found himself back in his room. He jumped up and peered out the window. He couldn't understand what had just happened, but he felt the best place to look for Filbert was at the foot of the maple tree.

Unfortunately, Filbert wasn't there and then he recalled the first time he traveled with Filbert. He remembered the Pimby told him to tell himself "My mind is open." Johnny immediately closed his eyes and quietly started saying those words over and over while picturing the white place in his mind. WHOOSH! Opening his eyes Johnny found himself back in the white space with Filbert, who was smiling with the biggest grin Johnny had ever seen. A grin truly from ear to ear.

"Congratulations, Johnny. I knew you would make it back."

"What happened?"

"Do you remember when I asked your permission to begin this the first time we met?"

"Yeah."

"Well, while I do not have to ask you anymore, you have to be as careful with your thoughts as you must be with your words, like I told you the last time I saw you. Your thought of 'forgetting about this and being in over your head' was a way of you taking away the permission you gave me. You see Johnny, when you doubt things - you start to lose confidence in your abilities and then you lose your ability to stand by your decisions. This then causes you to block the road to imagination. Here, in pure imagination, the main thought you hold in your mind can create an effect, which is what just happened to you when you returned to your world. In your thoughts of uncertainty, you secretly pictured returning home and your fear and worry were so strong that your unspoken wish came true. A good exercise for you is to tell yourself over and over 'I trust this process - I stand by my promise to be here'."

"Filbert, it's just that all of this is super confusing. Next time I am going to bring a dictionary! And there are so many rules, and everything seems so complicated", Johnny said sounding very discouraged.

"I know this is all very hard to accept," Filbert said to Johnny in a comforting voice.

"Johnny, think of it as you are learning how to drive - you first need to learn all the rules of the road and how a car works, right?"

"I guess so."

"Just trust me and the process, ok Johnny? I know it is a lot to understand all at once but to be perfectly honest Johnny, you are going much faster than anyone else I have ever worked with. Remember, we are just planting seeds. I know you were worried about 'tests', but for now recognize that sometimes, even though we use the same words, the definitions are different in my world. I come from a much different, more flexible world than you are used to - a world of unlimited possibilities. You will come to see in time that you and I actually come from the same world. I guess when I used the words 'life-long test', I should have said 'life-long discovery'. I bet that sounds better, right?"

"Phew!" Johnny said wiping his forehead with the back of his hand for dramatic effect. That does sound a lot better."

Just then the humming started up, though it seemed much different to Johnny in this place - in some way softer. Johnny had been trying to accept all the strange events that had happened since meeting Filbert but found what was happening at this exact moment to be just freaky.

The entire place started to look like liquid as the humming grew louder. The walls, the floor, and even the ceiling, all started to resemble milk. While he wasn't actually getting wet, he did watch his feet slowly start to sink into the floor. Soon the floor started to ripple and flow up over his ankles like the surf at a beach.

"Johnny you are free to ask anything you want because no question is ever stupid. Always ask your questions, even if you think they sound stupid. Questions are the only way you can grow and learn. And remember, no harm can ever come to you in the world of imagination, so don't be scared."

"Ok Filbert. Surprisingly I'm not scared but I've got so many things that I want to ask. What is the humming sound? Why does this place now look like milk? But my first thing I really want to ask is do you know what I'm going to ask you before I ask you?"

"Not really Johnny. I can tell when you have a question. I can feel your mind reaching out to me asking for help. It feels like your mind is knocking on my head. But I don't know what exact question you have."

"Ha! Ok. I just believed you always knew all of my questions before I ever ask them. That is why I never thought to ask because I believed it best to wait for you to tell me everything I wanted to know."

"Creation does not work that way, Johnny. You have to be active. You can imagine anything you want in your life, but it is not like putting on the television and everything is right there for you to watch. Instead, you need to adjust your antenna. You need to be the director of the scene - which over time, becomes the film of your life. It is the same with getting answers. You must step up and ask. Only by asking can you grow. Remember Johnny, you must be active in your life."

"Ok Filbert. I think I get it, well sort of."

"Johnny, I want to ask you to just relax about 'getting things', ok? This is a journey and there is so much that will only become clear with time. Have you ever seen a mosaic?"

"Yeah, actually my cousin Staci makes them, why?"

"That is great, you should go talk to your cousin about how she makes them, but let me ask you this - when you lay the first piece of the mosaic in the glue, what does it look like?"

"Ah, it really doesn't look like anything."

"Exactly Johnny, it is hard to understand the final picture with just the first few pieces, right?

"Yeah, I guess."

"Well, I want you to think about our journeys as if we are building a mosaic. In time, the picture will make sense to you."

"Filbert, seriously - and before you take out your brain from your little head – all of this makes my brain feel like it is in a blender."

"Ha-ha Johnny. That is good because my job is to shake up your world."

"Well then you are succeeding my friend!"

"So, Johnny, what were your other questions?"

"Oh yeah. What is this humming sound I always hear and why does it now seem we are somehow in a can of white paint?"

"Great questions. We are about to go on a journey, right?

"Right."

"Do you remember how the last time I asked you certain questions to take us to the place we needed to go."

"Yeah. Of course, how could I forget."

"Good. Well, your answers to my questions came from your imagination, but now we are in the world of pure imagination as I explained to you earlier. So, I can bring the experience to us. What is really happening is that the room is in the process of converting into what I want you to experience. In other words, the event will come to us. It is exactly what happened when you created your special place, even though you did not see the imaginative process in your mind. When you answered my questions what actually happened was very similar to you having had a white piece of paper in your head and slowly you started to put different colors and objects on it until it formed what I sent you to find. You can think of this place as the blank piece of paper in your mind. Does that make sense?"

"Yeah. It is like drawing or painting, but what you're saying is that here the painting shows up already finished, right?"

"Johnny, that is a rather good way to think about it. Try and think of it more like the ride at the amusement park your father used to take you to. Remember the ride where it felt like you were flying a rocket ship?"

"I loved that ride, but how'd you know my dad used to take me."

"Johnny, I may have only showed up recently, but we Pimbies keep our eyes on our future seedlings from the time they are born. Sometimes children are so connected to their imagination that they tell their parents about having imaginary friends. That is because they sense us even though they can't see us."

"Oh wow."

"Ok back to our rocket ship ride. If you remember when you first walked into the ride the room was completely dark, true?

"Yup."

"And it was only when the screens turned on that you actually felt like you were in a rocket. Well think of this place as that type of ride. The walls start off white but soon, when they turn on, you will be able to see what I want to show you."

"Cool. And is that why the walls are moving like liquid? Is it like those times when the satellite dish does not pick up a good TV signal and there's static before the picture comes on?"

"Exactly! Now you asked about the hum. You will have to take my word on this. If you want, you can go to a museum when you get home and test it out. I believe you have a great natural history museum in your city, right?"

"Yeah, but museums are boring."

"Well, I am sure you will want to go after I tell you about the hum. What would you say we are doing when we use our imagination?"

"Filbert, I don't understand the question. When we're using our imagination, aren't we imagining?"

"Yes Johnny, but try and be more…"

Johnny immediately interrupted Filbert already knowing the answer, "Flexible."

"Perfect Johnny. Yes, try and be more flexible. Let me ask you again. What would you say we are doing when we use our imagination?"

Johnny felt as if the wheels in his head were spinning so fast. He thought over and over about all the times he tried to imagine things but couldn't find an answer to the question. Then, without realizing it he closed his eyes and began repeating, "I am flexible."

He instantly pictured his special place and found himself walking up to the temple. Gazing at the golden pillars he felt the strong urge to touch one of them. He was surprised at how warm it felt. His right hand then sunk into the warm gold, and he instantaneously understood that he'd built this temple in his imagination. Excitedly he yelled out to Filbert, "Building! When we use our imagination, we are building things!"

"Wonderful answer Johnny. Give me another word."

"Uffa!"

"Flexible Johnny, flexible," Filbert said in a joking voice.

The word build swirled around in Johnny's head, spinning around like a tornado in his mind. He started laughing to himself about how funny it was that he created a tornado in his mind, and in that precise moment he knew in his heart of hearts the right answer. Looking at Filbert, he smiled and said, "Create."

"Now that was not so hard, was it, Johnny?"

"Says you," Johnny responded with a smirk on his face.

"Ok, so you figured out that when you use your imagination you build, you create. Well, you can think of the sound you hear as the engine of imagination, the machine of creation. Do you know what has the same sound?"

"A buzz saw, a jack hammer, a car engine", he blurted out. Despite being so eager to come up with answers, Johnny started getting annoyed and finally blurted out with a sigh, "Uh, oh, I don't know."

"Johnny, I know it is hard because you are not used to all of this but try not to get annoyed or frustrated - you don't want to pop back home, right? Remember to just go with the flow and be flexible. Plus, you could not have known this answer and that is ok. In your world people worry a lot about needing to always know the correct answer, but not knowing is useful because it keeps you learning. Imagine how boring it would be if you were on a treasure hunt and already knew where to find the treasure."

"Yeah, I guess you are right Filbert."

"Well, let me tell you the answer. It is your sun that makes the same humming sound. Next time you go to your science museum see if they have a recording of the sound of the sun. And the sun helps everything on your world grow, even you! In fact, without the sun there would be no creation."

"NO WAY!"

The humming sound continued getting louder and louder. The room no longer seemed to be flowing but instead started spinning like a waterspout. Johnny glanced over at Filbert who'd completely lost his cloud consistency. While he was still floating, he was definitely much more solid than before. Johnny was fascinated by how fast the walls, floor and ceiling were spinning, yet he was standing perfectly still and didn't feel the least bit dizzy.

SWISH, he heard and quickly turned to his right as a stream of red paint flew by. SWISH, then he saw a stream of green, then orange, then so many colors he couldn't keep track. One thing he knew for sure was that the egg-shaped room began shrinking. He focused on Filbert again, this time with a concerned expression on his face. Filbert just smiled and nodded, letting Johnny know to relax and that everything would be ok. A moment or two later the room turned into a funnel, the floor opened up beneath them and they were sucked into a black tunnel. Then - silence.

"Filbert," Johnny whispered. "Are you there? Where are we?"

"I am here Johnny. It will take you a moment for you to adjust to our new place. I want you to take the three breaths now and tell yourself you are flexible, and your mind is open. You are going to feel quite strange during this experience. Do not fight it - just let everything happen. Remember, you cannot be hurt here."

"Filbert" Johnny whispered again, "You're scaring me. What are you talking about? Why do you keep saying I won't get hurt?"

"Shh, Johnny, trust me," was all Filbert said.

Once Johnny's eyes adjusted, he swiftly realized there was absolutely nothing to see. He found himself in a completely dark, tight space. He was lying on his side with his body bent almost like the letter C. He also felt a sticky substance all around him. He was awfully uncomfortable and wanted to stretch but couldn't wiggle enough to get his legs and arms into a more comfortable position. He also smelled the smell of mud. But more than anything, he wished he were able to move his hands so that he could at least feel around this small space.

"Filbert, are you still here?"

"Yes, I will always be with you Johnny."

"What are we doing here?"

"It will all become clear soon Johnny. Trust me."

Johnny tried to stretch again. His legs started aching and he started getting a charley horse in his right calf muscle. This time he heard a cracking sound but couldn't make out what cracked and whatever had cracked certainly didn't let in any light. Soon after, he heard the sound of dripping water.

What in the world? Where am I? he thought to himself.

The dripping sound started getting louder and he began to feel water flow under his shoulder and also drip on his head. He was stunned that he didn't feel any fear. However, the sound of the water made him realize how incredibly thirsty he was. As some water dripped near his mouth, he rapidly stuck out his tongue and started to drink. The water was wonderfully cold and refreshing and for some reason also gave him a lot of strength.

After a few more drops, he felt strong enough to wiggle himself into a better position and stretch. The more he stretched, the more he felt the walls of this dark, tiny space expand. His legs were almost straight and every move he made produced greater creaking and cracking sounds.

Johnny became extremely energized by the possibility of getting out from this place. He had no idea where it would lead him or what would be next, but all he knew is he wanted to get out. He didn't let fear stop him. Something inside him told him to push again. "Stretch" he heard a voice scream in his mind. So, he stretched and stretched and stretched.

"WHAT THE HECK, FILBERT!"

"Relax Johnny. Go with it."

As Johnny continued to stretch, he felt his legs and arms getting longer and longer. Slowly they were making their way out of the tight space into what felt like paste. Even though he couldn't see, he knew he was getting very long. The strange thing was it started to seem natural for him to stretch like a rubber band. He had the strangest feeling that he'd been born to stretch like this. The water was flowing stronger now, and Johnny drank more and more, but his thirst didn't seem to go away. With each sip, he grew bigger, twice as big as before! Just when his arms and legs were almost done stretching, his fingers and toes started to stretch too. It felt funny, but somehow, started to really enjoy the feeling of his body stretching.

Much better than being cramped in that small space, he thought.

It seemed like he'd been stretching forever. Gradually he started to feel warmth around his fingers. The tips of his fingers felt as if they were getting close to a flame. At the same time his toes were definitely getting much colder. Neither the heat nor the cold felt like anything he'd felt before, but both felt very safe. At that moment, Johnny's neck began stretching, sending his head up through what he now knew was mud. Faster and faster his head moved in the same direction his fingers were stretching towards.

"Light, Filbert, I see light!"

His fingers broke through the surface first into a warm beautiful light. Gently they started to uncurl and stand straight up wanting to touch the light. Then his head broke through the soil. The light started to fill his whole body, trickling down through his fingers, through his head, down his arms, through his chest and heart, finally reaching his toes. Johnny was able to shake off the dirt remaining on the top of his head. When he looked at his fingers, he couldn't believe his eyes. He was a baby tree – a sapling.

To his amazement he didn't panic and instead felt a great sense of calmness. He felt his arms swaying with the wind as the sun shone over his leaves and trunk. It felt wonderful.

"Filbert, this is so strange. I feel so happy to be a tree. Why am I not afraid? Why am I not worried?"

"Johnny, you are happy because you are fulfilling your duty as a tree. You are connected to the purpose of a tree. A tree's job is to grow, to clean the air, to provide shade, food, a home for birds, stuff like that. Right now, in this moment of imagination, your mind does not know it is human. It believes it is only a tree and a tree does not have the ability to think or compare itself. It does not say to itself, "Oh, I wish I were a stone." It is simply happy being a tree.

Filbert continued, "What happens with humans as they age is that they forget about who and what they really are. They get caught up in gossip, which clothes to buy, how much money to make, all that stuff. They start to compare themselves to other people, wishing they were taller, skinnier, richer, had a car like their friend or a job like their neighbor. Humans are the only ones that have these negative behaviors of comparison, and it distracts them from how special they are. A Beagle does not complain because it isn't a Golden Retriever. A Finch does not wish it was an Eagle. A Dolphin does not compare itself to a Shark, as a tree can't wish it was a flower. Can you understand that?"

"Sort of, Filbert. I mean a tree doesn't have a brain, so it can't do those things." Johnny said with a little uncertainty in his voice.

"You are right Johnny, but what I want you to understand is that we each have a true nature, something unique. Remember how I told you that your uniqueness is part of your magic?"

"Yes Filbert, that was when I created my temple. You said my uniqueness is a source of my magic."

"You have an amazing memory Johnny, I am glad you were listening," Filbert said chuckling. "Well Johnny, comparing yourself to others destroys that connection to your magic. Do you know anything about Theodore Roosevelt?"

"You mean President Roosevelt, right Filbert?"

"Yes Johnny. He was a wise man and once said 'comparison is the thief of joy.' I want you to put his quote in that remarkable memory of yours and never forget that joy is also a source of magic. Can you do that?"

"Yes Filbert, but I still do not understand what this has to do with the tree."

"Thank you Johnny for keeping us on topic," Filbert said with a twinkle in his eye. "Right now, your human body is connected to one thing, being a tree, and is freed from other thoughts. It is free from comparison."

"Ok Filbert. I guess this is another thing that I will understand in time. You know, the list is getting long. But I can also ask my dad after I turn nine, right? He will be able to help me?"

"Oh yes Johnny. A parent's job is to help water these seeds I am planting in you. Now, you are about to feel many things. Remember, if you get nervous or worried, no harm can come to you."

The sun began to rise and set at an abnormally fast pace. Johnny perceived that time was speeding up because he felt himself growing much taller and wider. Rains came, snow came, his leaves turned colors, fell off and then new buds appeared.

This is so amazing! Johnny thought to himself.

He was now about 27 feet tall and could see for miles from this height. He had no idea where he was, but it didn't matter because he felt happy. The landscape was so beautiful, covered with lots of rolling hills and freshwater streams. He felt a tingling all throughout his many limbs. In no time he started producing apples.

Whoa! I am an apple tree!

Many animals came to his tree to feed on the apples. Insects ate his leaves. He was providing food for so many creatures and it made him feel so incredibly happy. While concentrating on how he was an apple tree, he didn't notice the town growing around him. Soon enough, he heard car horns honking all around.

Funny, he thought to himself, *I didn't realize people had moved into this area.*

Around that same time the air started to take on a more clouded, smoky, thick feeling. He soon understood it was the exhaust from the cars polluting the air. He knew that trees took in bad air and produced good air, because his father had explained it to him on one of their camping trips. His mom later told him in a more scientific way that trees take in carbon dioxide and release oxygen into the environment. Oddly, he felt out of breath.

"I'm a tree. I don't have lungs. How could I feel out of breath?"

Filbert, sensing Johnny was feeling slightly nervous, quickly answered his question even though Johnny hadn't directly asked him.

"Johnny, there is much more pollution in the air now than there had been when we started the exercise. As a tree, you are absorbing much of the pollution in order to produce clean air for the world. It is amazing how only a few cars can have such a big impact on the quality of the air. Wouldn't you agree?"

"Yeah, I agree Filbert, but I can't understand this. Is this how a tree feels? I didn't think trees had feelings and I know they don't have lungs."

"Johnny, you are feeling the effects of the pollution because while you are a tree, you are still a human boy inside the tree. It is the same thing you have been experiencing by being able to see even though trees do not have eyes, right? And trees do not have ears, but you have been able to hear, right? You are a human experiencing what it would be like to go through the cycles of a tree's life, but you still have your human feelings, understand?"

"Yeah, but, Filbert, do trees feel?"

"Johnny, remember how I told you words have different meanings in different worlds. Well trees do not 'feel' like humans think of 'feeling', but a tree can be affected by the place where it grows and 'feel' the effects of the environment. Scientists in your world have shown that trees can feel sensations. Studies show that plants can sense a touch as light as a caterpillar's footsteps."

"Wow. Ok, Filbert, that sort of makes sense. I guess I always thought thinking and feeling are the same thing. So, what you're saying is that trees don't know they're getting sick from things like pollution, even though they get sick."

"Exactly, Johnny."

"And you said I can't get hurt, right?" Johnny asked with a hint of worry in his voice.

"Definitely, you can never be harmed on our journeys, but you may certainly change your thinking after them."

During their conversation, many seasons must've passed because Johnny observed many new roads and homes built around the plot of land where he'd taken root. He also saw that the streams had become rather murky, and there were fewer animals around than there'd been before. While staring out over the land, he started to feel nauseous and as he looked down, he saw there was a farmer spraying some stuff on his leaves.

"Hey, get away from me," Johnny wanted to scream, but of course couldn't.

"FILBERT, I feel sick."

POP! Johnny and Filbert were back in the white room. Johnny, sitting on the floor, was rocking from side to side, moaning and breathing heavily. He then curled up like a ball holding his stomach. At that moment Filbert's white fur became very long, and he started shaking like a wet dog. Colors flew from his body like a sparkler, raining over Johnny. Within about nine seconds Johnny stood up.

"Filbert, what happened? I don't know what to ask first. I'm so confused. I guess I can start by asking…hmm." Johnny paused and then asked, "What did you just do?"

"I gave you some of my energy in order to quicken the process of your body getting rid of the feeling of the pollution."

"But you said I couldn't get sick. You lied!"

"Johnny, I did not tell you a lie. You were not sick - there was nothing physically wrong with you. It was the tree that had become sick. You just felt what was happening to the tree as it happened. Fear grabbed a hold of you, and you forgot that you were not really the tree. You let your fears trick you into believing that what was happening was actually happening to you. You are very brave Johnny. Many of the other children I have worked with do not ever get to this point. You just needed to remember that you were not a tree, that I was with you, that you were only in an exercise created in the world of imagination and remember that nothing could harm you here, as I had told you. I know that was a lot to ask of you, but it was important for you to understand the role fear plays in your life. Fear is one of the hardest things for a person to control. As a matter of fact, it is much easier for fear to control people because the human brain is programmed to protect you. Fear helped the first human beings survive from things like saber-toothed tigers, for example. Yet today, people let their fears stop them from doing many things and never really ask why they are afraid or if their fear is real."

"But when I was the tree, I knew I was sick, or the tree was sick. I don't know how to explain myself. What happened Filbert?"

"You are right. The tree became sick from all the chemicals and pollution. As you know trees produce clean air, but a tree is not a machine. It is a living creature and can only handle so much dirty air before becoming sick. That is what you experienced, the tree starting to sicken from all the pollution. Do you understand so far?"

"Yes Filbert."

Filbert continued talking, "Pollution results from something we call selfish imagination. Remember that imagination is a powerful force and can produce many great things for the world. Think of all the great inventions in the world, but it is when people do not think about the effects of their actions that their creations could cause serious problems for the world. Your world is experiencing a huge climate problem right now and many animals, trees and insects are dying that are all needed for the world. Investigate what is happening to bees for example. Humans forget that they did not create the world. The world was created by a greater power and is perfect just as it is and therefore should be respected. However, humans have allowed their imagination to become selfish and are trying to control and change nature. Humans are now destroying forests, building fake islands, drilling for oil in the oceans, and doing many things that have hurt the earth. Now the world must adjust. There is a word for when something needs to adjust to change. It is called adaptation, or some say evolutionary adaptation. Do you know what that means Johnny?"

"Ah-dapt-what? No, not really. Again Filbert, I really don't know what you mean. Can't you just pop a dictionary into my brain," Johnny said, only half-joking.

"Ha-ha Johnny, you are fun. Well you can think of it like this, adaptation is how something adjusts to changes. How something changes to survive in a new situation. You recently learned about a lizard called a chameleon in science class, right?"

"Yeah. It's able to change its color to hide from other animals that may try to hurt it."

"Exactly. That is a form of adaptation. Another example would be the Alaskan Wood Frogs. Get this Johnny, in the winter they can let their bodies freeze solid. They actually stop breathing and their heart stops beating. This allows them to survive the tough winters. And in spring, they thaw out and 'come back to life."

"That's insane."

"Crazy, right Johnny? You can think of adaptation, which I know is a big word, as adjusting to a new normal."

"You mean like with the pandemic? I heard on the news every night people talking about a new normal. Is that the same thing?"

"Yes, people had to adapt how they lived because of change."

"Ah, I think I understand it a little better Filbert, but what did you mean about evolution-something adaptation?"

"Well Johnny, right now the earth is going through a process of evolutionary adaptation to adjust to all the pollution and harm people have caused. Have you heard in the news that there seems to be many more tornados, hurricanes, earthquakes, and there are even more volcanoes that are erupting? Scientists say it is all part of the process of adjusting to a more polluted world."

"Yes, I have. I recently saw news coverage of a big earthquake in Italy. Does this mean the world is in danger, Filbert?"

"I actually cannot answer that question Johnny, because it is beyond my ability. I am not able to see the future because the future is in the hands of the people on earth. We come to guide all of you when you are young, but sadly, many people forget about our visit. That said, the future of the earth has always depended on how people act in response to what they have done to the earth. How they react to the consequences of their actions. The future of the earth will always be in the hands of human beings. A lot of improvements have been made. Did you know many years ago there was no such thing as recycling or that people were able to smoke on a bus, or that people would throw garbage away in the oceans?"

"No way. That's disgusting, I can't believe it, Filbert."

"It's true Johnny, you should ask your grandparents about what the world was like for them. The good thing is that people are now starting to wake up to the impact they caused to the earth and are now trying to take care of it. The future will require people to connect to their imagination to do good things and not be selfish."

Johnny studied Filbert for what seemed like a long while, trying to understand everything that had happened.

"Not all our journeys will be like this Johnny, but this was such an important lesson to learn. It is important to understand that your actions and the actions of all people bring about effects that reach far beyond their own backyards. This is a lot for you to understand and to be honest you will not get it all at once. Again, it is as if I am planting a seed in your mind. All these lessons will become part of you. Hopefully, as you get older, you will stay connected to your imagination and these seeds will sprout. As more time passes you will understand more and more and more. Just trust me on this one."

"I do Filbert, I do, and I plan never to forget these lessons," was the last thing Johnny said before waking in his room.

The Color of Imagination

Johnny was sitting on his beanbag chair facing his alarm clock. It was 12:23 a.m. and he knew in exactly 45 minutes he'd see Filbert again.

While waiting, he thought about how he hadn't seen much of his parents lately. It didn't bother him much, though. He felt a bit guilty about not missing them, but he also felt a bit relieved they hadn't been around. Ever since Filbert's last visit, Johnny had been feeling a little strange. He liked being alone, especially because he had so many questions swirling around in his head about almost everything.

Cathy was the first one that started noticing a change in Johnny and a few days ago had finally asked, "Johnny, I can't help but notice you are acting very differently lately. You're not your usual talkative self. May I ask you if something is bothering you?"

"No Cathy, nothing is bothering me at all. It's just that I've started thinking about lots of stuff that I've really never thought about before."

"What do you mean?" Cathy asked.

"I've started to think about how the earth gives us so much water, air, food, beaches, and places to play. I've just never realized it before and that makes me think of other things and on and on," Johnny explained to Cathy.

"That's a really grown-up thought Johnny. What made you start thinking about things like these?" Cathy asked.

Johnny started to panic and could feel his face getting red remembering Filbert's rules about not sharing his journey with others. Now he felt he was letting the cat out of the bag. He feared that if he let out his secret Filbert wouldn't come back. Yet, something told him to just think about his special place and there he would find his response. He took three breaths before answering Cathy. In that quick moment, while at his special place the right answer came to him.

"I guess it's because I'm turning nine and I've started to see things differently," Johnny responded. He felt himself relax a little because he knew in that moment, he hadn't told a lie. He'd been trying to be careful with his words as Filbert told him to be.

Cathy smiled and Johnny noticed a twinkle in her left eye very similar to a small rainbow. Then she said, "Maybe it is Johnny. Your mind is very flexible for someone about to turn nine."

Flexible, how interesting that she used the same word as Filbert, Johnny thought to himself.

At that moment he wanted to ask her if she knew about Pimbies, but his heart told him otherwise. He'd learned to start to trust his instincts over the last few weeks and felt it best to keep his curiosity to himself during this period. After all, "this was his journey" according to Filbert. Johnny just smiled and replied, "Thanks Cathy."

Even now, as he waited for Filbert, he couldn't shake the feeling that Cathy knew something, just as he was sure his dad knew more than he'd ever let on. He decided he would ask Filbert if Cathy and his father both knew about what was going on when they saw each other in several minutes.

Just then he started to hear the humming sound and glanced over at the clock. *12:59, I can't believe how quickly time passed.*

Even though Johnny tried not to, he couldn't help but fantasize about where they would go, what they would do and what they would see. He knew he shouldn't have expectations, but excitement got the best of him because he knew anything was possible when he was with Filbert.

He closed his eyes and started thinking about the tree exercise and thought, *what if I were a leaf*? After asking himself the question, he felt a strong desire to visit his golden temple. This time he immediately arrived at the temple without having to take three breaths or say, "I return."

Cool, he thought to himself.

As soon as he got to the temple, Johnny saw something amazing. The big doors to the temple's only room started glowing for the very first time. With each step closer to the doors, he began to hear the same humming sound that normally announced Filbert's arrival.

I've never heard the humming sound in this place before, maybe Filbert is behind the doors.

The vibration from the humming became so powerful that it shook Johnny's entire body. He slowly reached out to open the doors and as soon as he touched the knob he started to float.

"What in the world" he said to himself and quickly remembered to be "flexible."

He didn't want to lose this experience by becoming afraid. He seemed to be floating over a forest. From that height he saw that there was a wide S-shaped river running directly in the middle of the forest. He also saw many different types of animals, birds, and trees. Slowly he felt himself being pulled towards the river. When he glanced down, instead of his reflection, he saw he had turned into a leaf.

"WHAT," he yelled out in panic.

His fear got the better of him, which broke the magic of the experience, and he found himself back in his room. He turned to check the time, worried he might have missed Filbert. 1:07 a.m.

"Phew", he said out loud, wiping his brow.

What just happened, he thought to himself. *How could I become a leaf just by having a thought and without Filbert's help? What's behind the doors in my temple?*

Johnny had so many questions but before he could form the next question in his mind everything around him turned into a big white whirlpool that sucked him into the vortex.

"Hi Johnny. How have you been?" Filbert asked.

"Great Filbert. That was such a cool way to arrive."

"I knew you would like it."

"I really did Filbert and I'm so happy to see you again. You won't believe all the stuff I have to tell you", Johnny replied with a big smile on his face.

"I am also very happy to visit with you again. I am sure a world of changes is taking place for you Johnny, especially since I can see your connection to imagination growing inside of you."

"What do you mean, growing inside me?" Johnny asked with a puzzled expression on his face.

"Remember how you told me that your favorite color was orange?" Filbert asked.

"Yeah. You said it was the color of my imagination."

"Good memory, Johnny. Well, there is a light that all people have inside them. It is located roughly in the center of their chests, about where your human heart is. Most people, as they get older, let their light go out, but for you, as you have been connecting to your imagination, the light is beginning to shine. In fact, one time the world was filled with wonderful light and color. People called this Joy. Joy is stronger than happiness. You can think of Joy as a vibrant, colorful happiness."

"You know Filbert, my mom used to say on her birthday that she wished we could all always be joyful. She used to say happiness was fleeting, but joy always exists. She said Joy is an inner feeling we need to lean into. Honestly, I have never understood that. Anyway, she does not talk like that anymore, I think because she is so stressed."

"There are many reasons Johnny that people lose their connection to their imagination and joy, which results in their light going out. We will talk more about this but, your mom is right, joy exists inside each person. It is part of their light and the only way to keep their light bright is to exercise their imagination daily so to stay connected to joy. A wonderful American poet named Henry David Thoreau once said, 'This world is but a canvas to our imagination.' That quote says it all Johnny, you hold the brush in your hand, you have the color of your imagination, and it is for you to start painting."

Filbert then reached over and touched Johnny's heart center. "Johnny, as your connection to your imagination grows stronger, not only will your light grow brighter, but over time you will also begin to notice the light in other people who are connected to imagination.

"Really?"

"Yes Johnny."

"Wow, then my dad really does know about Pimby magic! Remember I told you about the time he played the frosted glass bowl. What did you call it, a … a singing bowl?"

"Ah, yes Johnny, the singing bowl. What about it?"

"Well, my dad told people something about a golden light, or to connect to a golden light and I think that means he must know about all this stuff, right?"

"Hmm Johnny, I think he must have told everyone to imagine their heart to be a gold egg shaped light because that is part of the ancient traditions of using the singing bowl. That specific instrument was created long ago to help people unlock their strength and creativity. Gold, as you know, is an extremely powerful color that helps people connect to their imagination. That is why I am so delighted that your special place is a golden temple, because it is enormously powerful. But Johnny, I cannot say that means he knows. He could have just read about it in a book, or whomever he bought the bowl from might have told him about the ancient traditions. As I already mentioned, you will have to find this out yourself, and you will know when the time is right to ask the question."

"Ok, but can people see this light shining from me? I think Mickey would really be freaked out and I'm sure my mom would rush me to the hospital. Imagine what the doctors would say!"

Johnny started laughing very loudly as he started thinking of a doctor coming into an exam room wearing a pair of sunglasses. In fact, the more Johnny thought about it, the more he realized how much more he laughed since meeting Filbert.

"Johnny, you are becoming more and more of a jokester. That makes me so happy," Filbert said while still chuckling at the image of a doctor wearing sunglasses. Then he continued. "Johnny, if everyone could see the light, then that would mean everyone was connected to their imagination, right?"

"Yeah, I guess so."

"And if that were true then Pimbies wouldn't have to come to your world and help people connect, right?"

"Yeah, that's true," Johnny said in a definitive voice.

"You see Johnny, only people that are truly connected to their imagination - to their special place - can see the light in others. If you continue to stay connected to your imagination and keep your mind flexible - I believe that by your ninth birthday you will see the glow in certain people and certain people will see it in you. Children that have not been visited by a Pimby can neither shine their light nor notice someone else's light until they make the journey you are making now, so you don't have to worry about blinding Mickey." Filbert said giggling.

"Now Johnny", Filbert continued, "you mentioned you had many questions or things you wanted to talk about so please tell me how everything has been since I saw you last?"

Johnny couldn't contain his eagerness. So many thoughts and questions raced through his mind that he felt he'd literally trip over his thoughts.

"Well," Johnny began, "I think my nanny Cathy knows something. She smiled at me recently in such a strange way. I know this is going to sound crazy, but I swear I caught a rainbow-colored twinkle in her left eye. I've been noticing a lot of rainbow splashes of light all over the place, mainly in my house. Filbert, does Cathy know about Pimbies or can she tell something is going on?" Johnny asked.

Then, just as Johnny was about to ask the next question he started to chuckle because he knew how funny Filbert would find it.

"And Filbert, I already know what you're going to say, but am I imagining these rainbows?"

Filbert indeed laughed, as Johnny had expected, at his asking if "he'd been imagining." As Filbert continued to laugh, he started spinning and bouncing in all different directions. Then he started expanding and contracting with each new laugh. Johnny fell on the floor laughing at the sight of Filbert filling with air and becoming quite large, then becoming teeny tiny, while bouncing all over like a pinball.

Finally, Filbert calmed down and turned to answer Johnny. "Well Johnny, as you know I can never tell you if anyone knows about Pimbies or if they know about your journey. Sorry, just the rules. It is just part of the process needed for you to become more aware of people and to learn about what makes them special. What I mean is that if you are always asking other people to explain someone else to you, you will never be able to truly see and know the person you are asking about. You will understand this more in time. For now, it is one of those concepts I need you to just accept. Ok?"

"Ok Filbert, but I've got to say, there are a lot of things you say I will know later, uffa. Anyway, I think I understand this. If I always ask other people about someone else, I will never truly be able to understand who they are. My opinion would always be based on someone else's opinion. I'd never really get to know the person because I'd see them through someone else's eyes, or something like that, right? I think that is what you meant."

"You got it Johnny."

"You know, my dad once told me that someone can never truly know another person until they walk in their shoes. He also explained that I could never ask someone to do the walking for me. Honestly, I really had no clue what he was trying to tell me, but it seems to make sense now. I guess it's like one of my friends riding a rollercoaster and then telling me how it felt. That's a lot different than me riding the rollercoaster myself. Is that the same thing you're trying to tell me?"

"Right you are Johnny. Your father is an incredibly wise man."

A big, broad smile came to Johnny's face thinking about having such a great dad. Just then, he started to feel a tickle in the center of his chest, something he'd felt often since meeting Filbert. As he looked down, he watched an orange light spark from the middle of his chest for a split second. Johnny jumped back and turned to Filbert.

"Johnny, imagination is also fueled by love and what just happened is that you felt such strong love for your dad that you immediately started to glow. Have you ever heard people say "Oh she is in love - look how she glows? Or have you ever heard how, when a woman is pregnant, people comment that she is glowing? That is because, in the past, they really did glow. Sadly, today most people do not see the glow, but they still use the phrase. A long time ago, when people used to be connected to their imagination, as I mentioned earlier, people actually saw the glow and that is where the saying today comes from."

117

Johnny didn't say anything, he just observed Filbert thinking how much different his world had become in such a short amount of time.

"Now, Johnny, you asked me if you were imagining the rainbows," Filbert said with a big smirk on his face.

"Well Johnny, something you will come to understand is you are constantly imagining. Every time you think about something, part of it is always based in imagination. Imagination is the fuel that allows you to plan for the future, understand the present and remember the past. Sometimes imagination can be fun and sometimes it can be scary, such as when you worry about a test in school. Your worry is because you are imagining bad things, like failing or getting a bad grade. When you remember something from your childhood and it makes you smile, that is also imagination because it is not happening now. Yet, your imagination has allowed you to re-live it again. That is why as you learn to connect to the power of your imagination you will have more control over your feelings. You are starting to put the pieces of this puzzle together, but we have a few more things to experience together before it will all fit into place. Between you and me, you are learning very quickly."

"Thanks, Filbert," Johnny said and once again a sparkle of orange shone from his chest.

"Filbert, what about the rainbows? What do they mean?"

"Johnny, you always have the answers. Why don't you go to your special place and ask the question and see what happens?" Johnny then closed his eyes. He noticed over the last week that he didn't have to do many of the things Filbert had originally taught him about traveling to his special place. It was gradually getting much easier for him to visit the temple as time passed.

Immediately he found himself in front of the grand temple. As always, it was so warm and sunny. All the animals now acted like his pets and whenever he returned, they would come running up to him. He used to be super scared when the elephants ran toward him. But now, he just laughed as they ran up to him and tooted their trunks when he arrived, signaling to the other animals that Johnny was home. The monkeys would offer him bananas, the fish near the waterfall would do backflips and the birds would chirp beautiful melodies and drop flowers from the sky.

Though this time he stood in awe at a new thing that was happening. The waterfall was roaring so strongly that it formed huge mist balls in the sky that floated towards him. These orbs then stopped between him and the temple. As the sun shone through the mist, the largest, brightest rainbow that Johnny had ever seen formed between him and his temple. He passed under it, all the while keeping his head tilted back so he could examine every inch of the rainbow. It looked so thick and solid, not at all similar to rainbows he'd ever seen at home. It made him think of the stained-glass windows of the church in the middle of Hopewell Junction. He finally just stopped under it to look at how beautiful it was.

This is awesome, he thought to himself, which was then promptly followed by a slight tickle in his chest. He glanced down, having just learned what the tickle meant, and as expected, he saw the orange glow sparkling from his chest. Somehow it already felt natural to him to see light shining from his heart. He began to chuckle looking at the light, which only made it shine more intensely. The brighter it shone, the more it tickled him, making him laugh more and more. His chest now glowed like a floodlight as he walked up the stairs to the large patio of the temple. *I must look like a walking lighthouse,* he thought to himself as he stood in the middle of the room.

The ceiling appeared to sparkle more than usual, which he figured was just his glowing light reflecting off the golden ceiling. Then he sensed there was something much different about the ceiling since the last time he visited. He wished he could get closer to the ceiling and suddenly he felt something push him from under his feet. He looked down but didn't see anything unusual so he turned back to stare at the ceiling wondering how he could get closer when he felt the same push again. It felt like something was poking at his soles. Then a thought popped into his mind causing him to say out loud in a very firm voice, "I want to float to the ceiling." At that moment, each foot started to inflate. Bit by bit he started to lift off the ground and began floating around the room.

This is the greatest thing ever!

He started to do a few spins in the air and let out the biggest "whoo-hoo", which echoed back at him. He then heard the whoo-hoo a second time and understood it wasn't at all an echo, but that the pillars of the temple were shaking and laughing with him. He then pointed himself towards the ceiling so he could check out what made it shimmer so much more than usual.

Slowly he approached the ceiling. He could see the ceiling wasn't solid like he thought. This golden ceiling was made of thousands of tiny little golden stars all bunched together like grapes that were twinkling. He couldn't help but smile at them and the more he smiled at them, the more they twinkled. *They know I'm looking at them. They know I really like them.* Without worrying about how foolish he'd look to people back home if they could see him, he said, "Hello twinkling stars. I'm so glad you are part of my special place."

Immediately they started blinking faster than he'd ever seen any light blink, faster than the fastest blinking Christmas lights.

In fact, the twinkling started to make a type of musical sound, which slowly became a very high-pitched voice saying, "Thank you."

"You're welcome," Johnny responded.

This new development made Johnny want to explore his special place a little longer, but he knew he needed to ask his question and get back to Filbert. "I'll be back," he said to the stars and then floated down and sat cross-legged on the floor, exactly in the middle of the room.

His heart continued to beat rapidly due to his excitement about the stars, so he decided to take a few deep breaths in order to relax and concentrate on his question. Then he closed his eyes and asked his question, "What do the tiny rainbows I'm seeing at home mean?"

He opened his eyes and found the entire room jam packed with rainbows. He had his answer. He thanked the temple and then pictured sitting with Filbert in his mind. "POP," he returned to the white room finding Filbert floating directly in front of him.

"Have a good time Johnny?" Filbert asked.

"I had a great time, Filbert. The temple is becoming more and more magical with each visit. And you wouldn't believe what the ceiling of the temple is made of."

"Johnny, I can believe everything because I think anything is possible. That is what my world is all about."

"Duh, of course you can Filbert, I forgot. Anyway, let me tell you - it is made of tons of stars, twinkling golden stars and they're alive, they even saw me and said 'thank you' to me. And you know what else?"

"What Johnny?"

Johnny then told Filbert about the rainbow when he first arrived, the orange light from his chest and how he'd actually floated up to the ceiling.

Johnny could tell that Filbert was incredibly happy because he started to spin wildly in the air.

"This is wonderful, Johnny!" he said as he continued to spin all around the room. "You are really beginning to understand and connect to both the power of your imagination and your special place - a place where anything is possible."

"So, tell me, Johnny, did you get the answer to your question about the rainbows?"

Johnny began to explain to Filbert how he'd sat on the floor, closed his eyes, and asked his question and when he opened his eyes the room filled with rainbows. "When I saw all the rainbows," Johnny told Filbert, "I knew then that they are signs that I'm letting the power of imagination into my life. What came to my mind was that the rainbows I'm noticing at home are like the gold stars I used to get on my homework in the first grade."

"Exactly Johnny," Filbert said with so much excitement.

Johnny couldn't help but feel incredibly proud of how much progress he was making, which made his warm orange light start to glow yet again.

Filbert continued, "It is the way the universe tells you that you are on the right path. It is also a sign for you to remember that the power of imagination is always there for you. The more you look, the more you will notice that the universe is always sending you signals to stay on the right path. Many people call these signals 'whispers' because they are so subtle. You will need to pay attention for them. Now, before we get ready to go on our next journey, tell me some more about what has been going on since the last time I visited you."

Johnny thought about the last couple of days and how strange he had felt – but there was one thing swelling inside him that he really needed to talk to Filbert about first that was making him feel like he was going crazy.

"Filbert, since the last time I saw you and after being a tree, I've wanted to take a lot more care of nature than I ever had before. I've been trying to recycle more, use less water, but I've also found myself staring at birds for hours, and when I'm watering the plants, I feel they're telling me they are happy. Then the other day I dug up a rock in my backyard while digging a hole for a new bush my dad had bought over the weekend. When I picked the rock up I got an unusual electric shock. But the really weird thing was that an image flashed in my mind of what our town looked like a long time ago. I've never really cared so much about nature before, and now it seems it is one of the only things I think about. Even more bizarre is that I feel like nature is actually trying to talk to me. Yet that's not all Filbert. One morning, get this, while I was gazing out my window at the tree where we first met, I noticed the leaves turn to the sun as it was coming up over the mountains and I swear the leaves were smiling. Oh, and another totally weird thing happened last week when we had a huge storm. I was staring out the window watching the rain pour down and I'm sure I saw little smiley faces in the raindrops as they passed by the window saying 'Wheeeee.' What's going on Filbert?"

"Johnny, I am so thrilled for you. Again you surprise me with your ability to connect so strongly to the magic inside you. It is an exceptionally difficult thing even for people who have been connected to their imagination for a long time to observe such things. Now, to answer your question it will be easier for me to show you what is going on than to tell you. But I can give you a hint. Do you want one?"

"Ah yeah! In fact, I wish you would give me hints every time you plant these crazy seeds in my brain."

Filbert then floated over close to Johnny's ear and whispered – "everything is connected."

Johnny jumped back the way people do when a mouse unexpectedly runs in front of them. He glanced at Filbert with a puzzled look on his face. He felt, as he often did when Filbert explained things, totally confused. "What do you mean Filbert? How can everything be connected? I just don't get it."

Filbert told Johnny that the only way for him to "get it" was for him to continue with these adventures. He then told Johnny to close his eyes and take the biggest, deepest breath he could. Johnny slowly inhaled and inhaled and inhaled until he felt he would pop. Filbert then instructed Johnny to hold his breath and think of a super happy memory. Johnny knew that any memory about spending time with his dad would make him feel super happy, but he decided to search his mind for something magnificent.

Quickly, a super special memory came to mind. Johnny remembered a time when he visited his grandparents, who lived in one of the tallest skyscrapers in Clear City. His Dad had brought him into the city for the big 4th of July celebration and they camped on the roof of the apartment building.

Johnny loved visiting with all his grandparents but rarely saw his maternal grandparents because they lived in Arizona. His mom had once explained that Grandma Anna suffered greatly from the cold and needed to stay in a warm climate. Yet, it was his paternal grandmother Maria from Catania, Sicily that held the biggest place in his heart. She was a petite, slender woman with very tanned wrinkled skin and very curly black hair. His grandfather, Antonio from Abruzzo, Italy, had a big belly and a booming voice. Despite grandpa Antonio moving to the United States when he was three, he still spoke with a thick Italian accent.

Nonna Maria was like no one else Johnny knew. She had all these fantastic ideas, liked to take the city buses to places she had never been "just because", and would pick dandelions in the backyard and other weeds and cook them explaining the earth was rich

Johnny always had the impression that his mom was not a big fan of his Nonna Maria because she would always tell him not to listen to all the crazy things she said. Over time it led him to start calling his grandma "Crazy Mary," which she adored.

"Johnny, you need to live life freely. You need to always try new things, not be afraid and not care if people think you are crazy – why do you want to be 'normal', be unique Johnny because there is only one Johnny Prospect and there will only ever be one Johnny Prospect," he remembered her telling him.

That 4th of July holiday, while on the roof, he and his dad pretended to be camping on a gigantic mountain and that the car horns were hippopotamuses, and the airplanes were gigantic prehistoric birds. They'd set up a big tent on the roof and stayed up incredibly late. In fact, his grandmother came up to the roof a few times earlier in the evening with pies and brownies. Johnny knew he had to be grinning from ear to ear thinking about that special camping trip. Filbert then instructed Johnny to open his eyes.

Johnny was a little surprised to find they were still in the white room. Johnny had visions that they were floating or doing something cool. He couldn't understand what was so special about holding his breath. He was staring at Filbert a little baffled when Filbert winked his eye and said in a loud deep voice, "Now Johnny, exhale."

When Johnny finished exhaling, he noticed his breath formed a small ball that was floating in front of him, with a bright orange glow. Filbert had moved to the left side of Johnny's face and explained to him that his breath was now full of positive energy because he charged his breath with the good memory.

"It is like plugging in your cell phone to charge the battery Johnny, but instead you charged your breath."

Johnny continued examining his breath. At first it seemed to be a ball of air no bigger than a grapefruit, which baffled Johnny because he felt he'd let out a lot more air.

"Here we go" was all Filbert said before the ball of air started to fill the entire room and then in the blink of an eye Filbert and Johnny were smack dab in the middle of a baseball field when, all of a sudden, a baseball flew right past Johnny.

"Filbert, are you nuts? We're in the middle of a baseball game. We can get hurt and aren't people going to think they've gone looney seeing a boy and a Pimby pop out of thin air?"

"Johnny, no one can see us, but how interesting you used the phrase 'thin air'. Just watch your breath as it travels through the air."

Johnny had forgotten all about his breath, which continued to expand. Slowly his orange breath approached the players. The pitcher was the first person to be engulfed by the now pale

126

orange glowing breath. As the pitcher got ready to throw the ball to the catcher, he took a deep breath. Johnny not only watched the orange glow get sucked into the pitcher, but for a moment Johnny felt as if he was the pitcher. He felt his heart race, wondering if he would throw a strike. Then the ball released from the pitcher's fingers and Johnny could feel the muscles burn in his own shoulder.

Johnny turned to Filbert who put his finger up over his tiny lips signaling HUSH. Johnny kept his question to himself and just continued to watch. As other people inhaled some of the orange air, Johnny got a glimpse of what these people were seeing and feeling. Filbert then told him to pay attention to the breath floating higher into the early evening sky. Johnny turned his head up to the sky and watched his breath swell and float away like a hot air balloon. It was then that they lifted off the ground following in pursuit of his breath.

Johnny was so excited to be flying, he turned back to see the baseball field getting smaller and smaller.

"Filbert this is so amazing, it's so much different than when I was floating around in my temple," Johnny said excitedly.

Then, still gazing down at the town and watching how small everything was becoming, he noticed that the trees were taking in his breath and for a moment shimmered with a faint orange glow before turning back to green. He turned and looked ahead and watched as the clouds sparkled orange for a brief moment as they mixed with his breath.

Johnny couldn't help himself and had to ask Filbert one more time, "Are you sure no one can see us?"

"Johnny this is between you, me, and the universe."

"Good. I think my mom would have a fit seeing me float away from home." They both laughed. Then Filbert told Johnny to keep his eyes on his breath in front of him.

Next, it started to rain, and he saw that the raindrops had a slight orange tint. As they fell into the river below, the river shimmered orange. Even the grass took on an orange glow for a second when it absorbed the rainwater.

They then started floating even higher. The higher they floated, the darker it became, which made it easier for Johnny to see the orange mist of his breath in front of him. Soon they passed the moon, then other planets, and very quickly they were approaching the sun. As they passed the sun, he saw his breath surround the sun, which caused large solar flares to erupt from the sun's surface. He knew what a solar flare looked like from a movie he saw in his earth science class. From the tip of the solar flares, he witnessed orange-colored sparks headed for the earth – the same color orange that comes from his chest – the exact same color of his imaginative power.

"This is awesome," Johnny whispered to Filbert who was flying on his right side like a co-pilot. "I feel so special being here with you and seeing all of this. Am I right that the sparks that just left the sun are due to my breath reaching the sun?"

"Yes, you are 100% correct Johnny." Filbert explained to Johnny that the sun used the energy in his breath to radiate an extra burst of light to the entire universe.

"Filbert, I think this can go on forever," Johnny said softly as they approached the Milky Way.

POP! They were back in the white room.

"Filbert, that was incredible, and I didn't even feel afraid – not even a little. I always wanted to know what it felt like to fly. My dad has taken me on planes and helicopters, but this was the best thing ever!"

"I am glad you enjoyed it, Johnny."

"But Filbert, what happened? Why did it end so quickly?"

"Johnny, when you said it could go on forever, I knew you understood the basic lesson of the journey, so there was no reason to continue."

"You mean it does go on forever?"

"Well Johnny, without really knowing it, you figured it out. Breath, just like anything you do, is a type of energy and energy goes on forever. Energy can never be created or destroyed. That is why you always want to be careful with any type of energy you send into the universe. That includes your thoughts, your words, and your actions. We use breath in this exercise as a symbol of universal energy, because it is easier for a seedling to understand. All those things represent your energy. But there is something else that happened that is especially important. Do you remember the secret I whispered to you earlier?"

"You said everything is connected, but I have to tell you I'm still totally confused at what that means. None of this has made it any clearer to me."

"That is ok, Johnny. This is an adventure of learning and of changing the way you see things. Learning takes time and requires patience. Remember there are no stupid questions, and you can only learn by not knowing something at the beginning. Can you try and explain to me what you think happened with your breath?"

Johnny thought about all that had just happened. He thought about how he'd been able to see through other people's eyes when they breathed in some of his breath. How the trees seemed to glow for an instant with the same color as his breath. While he was able to tell all of this to Filbert, he couldn't figure out what "everything was connected" meant.

He closed his eyes for a moment and found himself standing in his golden temple looking into the stillest pond he had ever seen, so still in fact, that it looked like a mirror. He then noticed something next to his right foot, a shimmering orange stone that looked like a diamond. He was just about to bend down to pick it up when it leapt into his right hand. Guessing he was meant to throw it into the pond, he tossed it up into the air and it landed directly into the middle of the water. Then, in the reflection of the pond he saw all the things that just happened on his journey with Filbert through the orange-colored rings that came from the center of the pond where the rock had landed. He quickly pictured being back with Filbert.

"Filbert, I think I know the answer, but can I ask you something?"

"You can always ask me anything Johnny. What is it?"

"When I close my eyes and go to my temple I feel I must have my eyes closed for a long time. That makes me nervous to do it in front of other people because I must look like an idiot or look like I fell asleep. When I close my eyes and think of my temple, how long am I there?"

"Johnny, that is an excellent question because it must be something that stops you from using this tool more often. It is always good to remove anything that prevents you from connecting to your imagination. Johnny, the truth is that it seems like a fraction of a second to people in your world. It's unnoticeable."

"Phew, I'm so glad I asked. Thanks Filbert."

"Now, Johnny you were going to tell me what you figured out about our trip, right?"

"Oops," Johnny said placing his hands on both sides of his face. He felt a little embarrassed that he'd forgotten but just giggled about forgetting and then explained to Filbert about the pond in his temple.

"So, it isn't that we are all connected like a magnet to a piece of metal or something like that, but that everything I do has an effect on everyone and everything in the entire universe. If I litter, that piece of paper might go into a river and make a fish sick. If I help someone, then they may help someone else. But there's always an effect, sometimes it is a small effect or sometimes a big one, but there's always an effect, right, like ripples in a pond?"

"Terrific, Johnny," Filbert said in a loud, bellowing voice before spinning high in the air out of excitement.

"Johnny, have you learned about a guy named Isaac Newton yet in school?"

"Sure Filbert, isn't he the apple guy with gravity?"

"He certainly is, but do you know what his Third Law of Motion is?"

"His what?"

"His Third Law of Motion, you will surely learn about that when you take Physics, but that Law states that for every action in nature there is an equal and opposite reaction. He was a very wise man and that is exactly what I wanted you to learn from this exercise. You are truly brilliant Johnny, because your example of littering is a good example of what our friend Isaac meant."

"Wow, thanks Filbert. Can I ask you another question?"

"Always Johnny."

"I noticed that everything my breath touched glowed orange for a moment, does that always happen and we just can't tell on earth?"

"Johnny, you noticed the orange glow because this voyage only considered YOUR effect on things but remember there are billions of people on the earth, all with their own color. And as you know when all colors come together, they form white, so it is not noticeable on your earth."

"Hmm, ok that makes sense," Johnny replied.

"But there is something that you will notice as you connect more to your imagination," Filbert continued. "You will see whether the effect you cause is positive or negative. You will notice that because things will either grow brighter or become dull depending on… hmm, maybe it would be better to show you an example. Ok?"

"Sure"

Johnny instantly found himself standing in front of a field of sunflowers with Filbert at his side. The air felt so silky and pleasantly warm to Johnny. The landscape was unbelievably lush with very tall, skinny, pine type trees. He recognized them as trees normally found in Italy because his dad used to read travel books to him about places Mr. Prospect visited on business. Standing in front of the large field of sunflowers, Johnny couldn't help but wish his dad was there with him because he'd promised, that one day, his whole family would travel to Italy. This thought made Johnny so happy that the orange glow started to project from his chest. In that moment, the sunflowers appeared to become a brighter yellow. He was astonished at how extremely beautiful the flowers really were.

Johnny turned to Filbert, who smiled back at him and said, "See the effect you have on that which is around you. Johnny, because you feel so happy, you are actually projecting your happiness. The flowers are now picking up on that energy, and as they absorb some of your positive energy, they reflect it back."

"That's amazing, Filbert! Will I notice this at home, or only in places you take me to?"

"Johnny, if you stay connected to the power of your imagination you will begin to see this all the time, but you will also see the opposite, which is what I want to show you now."

"The opposite?" Johnny asked in a puzzled tone.

"I will show you Johnny. Now I want you to do exactly what I say."

Filbert then gave Johnny instructions to think of something that made him extremely angry, something that made him just want to scream and shout and throw things about. Johnny had to think for a while because since meeting Filbert he really didn't feel angry much anymore.

Finally, he remembered how last year his father had missed his birthday party because he had to stay in the city. He remembered being so angry that he pushed all his presents off the table. It then dawned on him that he hadn't even blown out his birthday candles because he stormed out of the dining room and went to his room slamming the door. As he thought about it, he observed the sunflowers were losing their brightness and started becoming slightly grey and dull. Filbert then started to whistle a beautiful melody. Johnny felt his sadness and anger evaporate and – POP – they were back in the white room.

"Did you understand, Johnny?" Filbert immediately asked.

"I think so, Filbert. I know that I affected the flowers because I felt angry, but did I hurt them in some way?"

"It is not that you hurt them Johnny, but if you think of being happy as positive energy, then being angry would be negative energy. Negative energy is like a dark cloud or smog that makes everything seem dull. You can think about how many times in movies you see the good guy is dressed in white and the bad guy in black."

"Yeah, at least in some of the science fiction movies I like, the bad guy is always dressed in black."

"If you noticed, the orange glow was not radiating from inside you. What you cannot see when you are in a state of negative energy is the grey colored beam that you send out into the world," Filbert explained.

"Why can't I see the grey Filbert?"

"You can never see the grey in yourself when you are angry or sad because you are no longer connected to the power of your imagination. You can only see when others are in a state of negative energy, of which sadness and anger are only two examples."

"What are other examples of negative energy, Filbert?"

"That is for you to figure out as you get older. If you stay connected to your imagination you will see grey in others. If you pay attention to what they are doing and how they are feeling you will be able to figure out what is positive and what is negative. I can only give you two major examples. Those are just the rules."

"Ah, the rules again," Johnny said with a disapproving expression on his face.

"Johnny, have you ever heard people say things like they feel so good around a certain person or that others seem to suck the energy out of the room?"

"Sure, I've heard friends of my parents say things like that. I've also heard things like that on TV. I've even said I feel good around certain people like Mickey or my grandmother. Why?"

"Because that is the effect of positive and negative energy or the way you will see it, bright and dull light. I am sure you have heard people say things like, 'Ugh, he was in such a bad mood that it brought me down.' That is because everything is connected and the strongest energy in a room takes over and affects everything. It is the same on a worldwide level, the more pollution, the more crime, the more sadness, the more people, plants, and animals will feel down and become dull. Does that make sense now?"

"I get it Filbert. I really get it. Thank you!!!!"

Johnny felt as if he'd just won a trophy. The glow from his chest erupted with such force that he felt himself lift off the ground and slowly spin, coloring the entire white room with orange light. He knew he made a major breakthrough. It made him feel so proud that he was learning how his actions could affect other people and things. He felt, in that moment, utterly confident that he'd never lose his connection to the power of his imagination. He was steadily understanding that imagination was in reality the power of his heart.

"Johnny, you mentioned you felt like the earth was trying to communicate to you, right?"

"Yeah."

"Do you understand now that it is reacting to you because you are developing a stronger connection to your power of imagination?"

"I do, sort of. But what about the electric shock from the rock?"

Filbert explained to Johnny that rocks, being the oldest objects on the earth, contain both a lot of history and a lot of energy. He also told him that there are certain Asian traditions that consider rocks to be teachers of important lessons. He then went on to tell Johnny that some of the power from the Pimby world rubs off on him each time he comes to the "white space", which causes him to see and feel things more like a Pimby and less like a boy.

"When I bring you in and out of my world," Filbert started, "you get dusted with Pimby magic and this allows you to feel magical energy most people can't. Nature is enormously powerful as it was created by something greater than the human imagination and you are getting to experience a connection to universal imagination each time we are together."

Johnny looked saddened for a moment and then asked Filbert, "Will it all end after the visits are over?"

"Johnny," Filbert replied, "for some it does and for others it does not. It all depends on how strong a connection you make during our time together."

"Ah, ok. I don't want it to end."

"Johnny, stay focused on our time together. The future does not exist at this moment, so don't worry about it now. OK?"

"Ok Filbert."

Filbert then let Johnny know that this visit was coming to an end. "Johnny you are learning so quickly, and I believe you will notice much more than you ever have over the next several days. Always remember to be flexible and keep your mind open," was the last thing Filbert said before Johnny found himself back in his bed.

He jumped out of bed to open the window screen. He stuck his head out to enjoy the cool breeze of the night air when he heard Filbert's voice whisper in the wind! "Everything has its own voice, Johnny."

I wonder what he means by that, Johnny thought to himself before climbing under the covers and falling quickly asleep.

Mistakes

Mickey finally found Johnny sulking in his room. "Dude, I've been calling out to you forever. What's up? How come you didn't answer me? I've been waiting downstairs for 15 minutes. Did you forget we had plans to go for a long bike ride this morning?"

"Why bother?" Johnny said in a glum voice before burying his face deep in his pillow.

"Bro, what's wrong? I've never seen you so down like this before."

"Nothing" Johnny answered. "Really Mickey, I just feel like being alone."

Johnny started thinking in the back of his mind, *how can I talk with Mickey? No one can ever understand.*

Johnny had become terribly upset over the last few days because he felt he was losing everything Filbert had taught him. He also felt very alone, like he had no one to talk to. He'd even stopped visiting his golden temple and as each day passed, he became angrier and angrier because he had no idea when Filbert would visit again.

Instead of leaving, Mickey sat on the bed and asked Johnny, "Are you mad at me for laughing when you did a belly flop into the pool instead of a dive at swim class the other day?"

"Not really, Mickey," Johnny mumbled into his pillow. Then, he slowly raised his head and said, "I know it was funny, but lately I'm making a ton of mistakes, and they always seem to happen in front of someone. It's embarrassing."

"It's funny too," Mickey snickered and for a slight moment glimpsed a small smile on Johnny's face. "At least your bathing suit didn't come off. Remember what happened to Paul last year when he came out of the water from his high dive? Now that was embarrassing!" Mickey bellowed.

Now Johnny had a full-fledged smile on his face. Mickey then picked up the other pillow and hit him over the head with it. Within no time he and Mickey were in the middle of a fierce pillow fight. The final blow was delivered by Mickey when his pillow suddenly tore open. As the feathers fell to the ground both Johnny and Mickey spotted a strange colored feather. Mickey immediately dove across the bed, picked it up and asked, "What type of bird do you think this orange feather with green zebra stripes comes from?"

"I really can't think of any bird that has such strange feathers," Johnny replied, all the while knowing it was his feather and Filbert would be visiting later.

"Yeah, who knows, maybe all these feathers are fake. Now, come on Johnny, it's a beautiful day outside and the summer is almost over - let's go for our ride."

Johnny had already started feeling a lot better after Mickey cheered him up, but it was knowing Filbert was on his way that made him feel super energized. He leaped out of bed, changed his clothes and he and Mickey hopped on their bikes towards the center of town for some ice cream.

They spent the rest of the day talking about going back to school, the girls at swim class, and Mickey's upcoming vacation with his parents. Johnny felt a little jealous because his mom recently told him that he needed to stay home this year and couldn't go on vacation with Mickey. He guessed it was probably best anyway because of his visits with Filbert, though he was also upset because his own parents had been so busy this year that they decided to cancel their own family summer holiday. Yet, in the end, Johnny figured that his trips with Filbert were more or less like going on vacation.

Later that night, Johnny told Cathy that he preferred to eat a sandwich up in his room instead of a full dinner.

"Sure Johnny, I assume you want bologna with mayonnaise?"

"Cathy, that would be great. Could you crush some potato chips in the sandwich and squash the whole thing like you used to do when I was a kid?"

"Of course. I guess you're not a kid anymore as your ninth birthday is almost here," Cathy responded with a rainbow flash of light in her left eye.

Johnny headed up the stairs with two sandwiches and a bottle of Coca-Cola. Usually his parents wouldn't let him drink soda, especially at night, but Cathy handed him the bottle saying it would be their secret.

After a few bites of his sandwich, he started thinking about all the things that had gone wrong over the last few days. Not only had he messed up his dive at swim class, but he also fell off his skateboard into the bushes in front of a group of girls he went to school with. He answered a bunch of math questions wrong and even the wheels fell off the go-cart he built for cub scouts. *What's wrong with me* repeated in his mind before falling asleep.

Johnny woke with a fright thinking he'd missed Filbert's visit only to find himself in the white space.

"Hi Johnny," Filbert said with a great grin on his face.

"Hi Filbert. I was so afraid I missed you because I fell asleep. I've been so down and tired lately," Johnny said with a sleepy tone of voice.

"You have too many worries, Johnny. You need to have more faith and not worry so much. You forget my world does not function like yours. Instead of worrying, maybe you could have just believed that I would make sure we visited with each other."

"I guess so Filbert, but so many things have gone wrong lately. I've made so many mistakes and it's been so long since we saw each other. I truly started to wonder if you were coming back at all."

"Johnny, you and I have a contract. I am your Pimby and must visit with you a set number of times. Those are the rules, but there is a reason why it took me some time to finally visit. Do you want to know why?"

"Of course I do," Johnny said very crossly.

"Well then, let me tell you. It was because you removed yourself so far from your imagination that I had to wait for you to allow some fun back into your life to visit. You finally opened the door for me when you stopped sulking and started playing again. It was only when you started laughing with Mickey during the pillow fight that I knew you were ready for my next visit. I can always force the door open if needed but I wanted you to understand the consequences of being detached from your imagination. You needed to see the difference between being positive and being negative. When you are negative, like you were because you were feeling so bad about things going wrong, you closed yourself off. Your orange light turned grey, and I waited for you to change your energy and turn your light back on. It is easier for me to travel to you when you are all lit up like a lighthouse," Filbert said with a giggle.

Johnny also giggled, picturing himself like a lighthouse with an orange light that Filbert needed to find. Johnny promptly recognized, in that moment, that this was the first time he imagined something positive or fun in quite a while.

"I understand Filbert, but you don't know how stupid I looked in front of people or how many mistakes I made these past few days. It was like everything was going wrong and I started getting so mad. I thought things were supposed to get easier and more fun now that you are in my life."

Filbert gazed at Johnny with a puzzled look on his little chubby face and then asked him, "What gave you that idea? Did I ever say or imply any such thing to you?"

Johnny stuttered to get his words out. "Ah, uh, oh, no, no Filbert. No, not really. It's just that we have so much fun together and I thought that's what should be happening all the time. I thought because I'm connecting to imagination, that everything would be easier - like magic."

Filbert's eyes widened to the point where Johnny could no longer see Filbert's nose or mouth. Then Filbert took his tiny left hand and stroked the long hairs on his chin. Then he unexpectedly started bouncing around the room.

Johnny started laughing so much that his sides began to hurt and just then Filbert stopped and said, "I have the perfect idea of what to do on this visit, but first I want to talk to you about your expectations that everything should now be fun."

"Again, with expectations," Johnny huffed. "What do you mean this time Filbert?"

Filbert began to explain to Johnny that he blocked the flow of imagination because he expected things to go in a certain direction. "Imagination is like a river Johnny. It flows. When you have expectations on how things are supposed to be, it is like building a dam in the river, which stops the river from moving naturally. Once you do that, you - in a flash - take the fun out of it instead of letting it be a kind of surprise. You disconnect from curiosity. You begin to think it should be one way and one way only or else you define it as wrong, bad and no fun. You try and control the outcome and put all these labels on everything, which then makes it feel like work. Johnny, it decreases your motivation because everything becomes hard."

"Are you with me so far Johnny?"

"I think so," Johnny replied. "It's more or less like what I saw on that game show after we first met. The one where the guy was disappointed because his car wasn't the color he expected, right?"

"Well Johnny, that is an example of a type of expectation, so yes," Filbert said while clapping at Johnny for coming up with an answer so quickly. "But there are other ways expectations can stop the flow of imagination such as when you are on a picnic and are expecting it to be sunny all day. Then a rain shower comes, and you get in a bad mood, but that is nature - let it flow. It is also like how some children expect to color perfectly in the lines and when they don't, they get upset. Yet, if they were to examine their picture, they would understand that it is unique because no one else has a mark outside the line in exactly the same way. Expectations block you from the magic flowing through life. There are many of these examples and your job will be to watch for them as you grow and not fall into the trap like you did these last few days. As you learned, it resulted in you being removed from your imagination. In fact, you detached from the fun in your life all because of your expectations. Being curious is much more fun than wanting things to be a certain way. I know you have a saying in your world that 'curiosity killed the cat.' This is not true at all; curiosity makes the cat's life fun."

Just at that moment Filbert turned into a cat dressed like Sherlock Holmes, with a big magnifying glass in his right paw causing Johnny to giggle.

"But Johnny," Filbert continued, "there is something else that caused you to be blocked and that is how you started focusing on 'mistakes' - focusing on what you call 'wrong'. That type of action drains you of your imaginative energy so quickly. I am now going to tell you a powerful little secret. Do you want to hear it?"

Johnny stood up in a rigid manner with a gleam of excitement in his eyes and leaned in toward Filbert and said in a low whisper, "Of course."

Then Filbert started to inflate like a hot air balloon. Soon Filbert filled basically the entire white space and then in the deepest voice Johnny ever heard in his life, Filbert said, "THERE ARE NO MISTAKES." The wind that came from Filbert's voice nearly blew Johnny over and the whole room seemed to shake.

"That isn't true Filbert. You told me you'd never lie to me!" Johnny said furiously while stamping his foot.

"If I add 2+2 and write 5 as the answer, I'm going to get it wrong on a test. It'll be a mistake, it'll be an error, and it will be something wrong!!!" Johnny felt so upset and could feel his face getting red. In that exact moment, Johnny witnessed that the entire room started to turn grey because of his anger. He took a few slow, deep breaths and the room returned to its bright white color.

"Good job," Filbert said. "I am glad you paid attention to your light. You catch on very quickly indeed. You were about to completely disconnect from the power of imagination and pop back into your room."

Johnny didn't respond. He remained very puzzled by what Filbert had said about mistakes and couldn't help but think Filbert lied to him.

"Johnny, I did not lie. Yes, it is true that 2+2=5 would be the wrong answer. Yet, it is not a mistake like you think. It is all a matter of perception. Do you know what I mean by perception?"

"Filbert, first I still feel annoyed. I truly am trying to be open to what you're saying and understand, but it is all so hard. And yes, I do know what perception means, but no matter what my perception, 4 is the right answer and only 4."

"I am glad you are trying to stay open Johnny. If you weren't, anger would have gotten the best of you by now and you would have popped away. Then I would have to fish you back like a salmon going the wrong way in a stream. Can you imagine a chipmunk fishing?" Filbert asked trying to make Johnny laugh a little.

Seeing Johnny still had a very stone-cold face, Filbert continued.

"Yes Johnny, but what I mean by perception is this, you can either call 2+2=5 wrong or you can call it an opportunity to learn the right answer. If you don't get something wrong, if you don't make mistakes, you cannot learn something new. Instead of the word mistake, which in your world is such an ugly negative word, I am suggesting you can think of it as a 'not yet moment.' You can just accept you have not learned it yet and that there is nothing wrong by still learning something. Your

146

world is too concentrated on things being perfect, but Johnny there is never perfection, there is only the pursuit of improvement. But let us save that for another time. For now, I want you to keep in your mind that you can only ever do your best in any moment, and if you need to try again, so be it - just concentrate on your effort to learn, Ok?"

"Ok Filbert, but I'll be honest, it sounds like you're talking a totally different language and I'm having a hard time understanding."

"Of course, Johnny, you are learning. Remember, I told you at the beginning that I would be stretching your mind, like Silly Putty, right?

"Yeah, but this one is really out there my friend."

"I know, just let it sit and percolate. Do you like kaleidoscopes Johnny?"

"I love them. Mickey has one. I don't. And it is so cool. Why Filbert?"

"I want you to think of perspective as a kaleidoscope. With one turn of the dial everything changes. Turn the dial in your mind's eye and a mistake can become a learning opportunity, ok?"

"Beh. Ok Filbert, but it is not that easy because I hate looking stupid in front of people."

"Well Johnny, change is always a bit uncomfortable, but it becomes easier the more flexible you become. Remember, everyone makes mistakes. You want to learn and grow, right?"
"Yes Filbert."

"Well, mistakes allow you to grow. So next time you feel that feeling of being stupid, why not say to yourself, 'Wow another thing to learn.'?"

"Ok, I will try it, but you know, it seems like a strange thing to do."

"Of course it does because you are used to feeling bad for not knowing everything, but from what I know, you are only almost nine years old. How can you know or be good at everything? Right?"

"Yeah, you are right. My Dad used to tell me all the time, 'Johnny, if you knew everything, you would be so bored. It is learning new things that makes life interesting.'"

"Johnny, I know I have said this before, but your father is a very wise man."

Johnny beamed with pride, so much so that his orange light blinded Filbert, who put on a pair of sunglasses that magically appeared out of thin air.

"Now, can I tell you another secret?" Filbert asked while sliding the sunglasses down his tiny little chipmunk nose.

"Sure, but don't blow me over this time," Johnny said slightly jokingly to Filbert.

Filbert rejoiced to see that Johnny started joking again and knew he had turned the corner. His anger was finally going away. He smiled back at Johnny before telling him the next secret.

"Some of the greatest inventions and discoveries frankly came from mis-takes."

"Really Filbert, can you name some?

"I could name many Johnny and believe they may actually surprise you. But do me a favor from now on, think of the word mistake as two words, mis and take, which means you just need to do something again. Ok?"

"Yeah, ok, if you want, but I totally don't get, as usual, what you're talking about. Now, weren't you going to give me some examples? I can't wait to learn about them."

"Sure Johnny. Did you know that Coca Cola started as a mistake?"

"Wow! Really Filbert?"

"Yes, a long time ago, a pharmacist named John Pemberton was working on a new headache medicine. He wanted it to taste good, but also to feel good. After working hard on the formula, he sent it to the medical board for approval when he thought he had finally perfected his concoction. When the examiners were inspecting it, they realized that the medicine tasted better than it worked. Today as you know it is the most famous soft drink in the world. Medicine it is not."

Filbert went on to explain that the potato chip was accidentally invented when a cook named George Crum got incredibly annoyed with a complaining customer who kept sending the french fries back to the kitchen for being too soggy. The chef then sliced the potatoes paper-thin, fried them for longer than he ever fried a potato before that moment, and sent them to the customer. That was the day the potato chip was born. He also told Johnny how Popsicles were invented by Frank Epperson when he mistakenly left a drink outside overnight and the temperature froze the drink with a spoon in it.

"Filbert, please tell me more."

"Thanks to Ruth Wakefield," Filbert began, "chocolate chip cookies were invented in 1938. While mixing a batch of cookies, she found that she did not have any baker's chocolate. As a substitute, she broke some sweetened chocolate into small pieces and added them to the cookie dough. She had expected the chocolate to melt and spread throughout the dough, making them chocolate cookies. When she took the pan out of the oven, she was surprised to see her idea did not work. She had accidentally invented the chocolate chip cookie."

Filbert explained that other examples included Teflon used in frying pans, plastic, penicillin and even Play-Doh, which was meant to be a wallpaper cleaner.

"Filbert, this is totally insane."

"Johnny, you know who Thomas Edison was, right?

"Sure"

"Good, well do you know that he made 10,000 of what you call 'mistakes' before inventing the light bulb? Imagine if he would have given up at 9,999 tries. See Johnny, he viewed a mistake as a period of 'not yet' and just kept trying."

"Neat!" Johnny said, with a look of astonishment in his eyes.

Soon the room began to fill with swirling colors. Johnny thought about how lucky he was to be learning all of this and couldn't imagine ever forgetting it. *It really is learning that makes life fun*, popped into his mind. Though, he quickly realized that people must forget all of the things they learn with their Pimbies because, if they remembered, the world would be a very different place.

How could anyone ever forget about their own powerful imagination, he thought to himself. He then laughed sarcastically under his breath reminding himself that he'd actually forgotten about his connection to imagination over the last few days. He was guilty of giving into fear, worry, self-judgment, and negative thinking.

Yes, he thought to himself. *That's what must happen. People must become overwhelmed with worry, fear, and judgments until negative thinking becomes so normal that they don't even realize that they have turned grey.*

He promised himself right then and there that he'd always do his best to stay connected to his imagination; that he'd always try to be positive and be careful with his words; that he'd try to avoid having expectations or judge things as mistakes but look at them as periods of "not yet," just like Filbert asked him to.

He was so immersed in his train of thought that he didn't realize the swirls of color had stopped and he and Filbert were standing in a hallway. Immediately, without having to even look around, he knew exactly where he was just by the smell.

He was standing in the hallway of his first home, the apartment in Clear City. He'd forgotten about the Italian family that lived down the hall that always seemed to be cooking pasta sauce, which made the whole hallway smell like tomatoes, garlic, and basil.

As he looked around, he couldn't believe how much he'd forgotten: the green and tan carpet, the striped wallpaper, even his own apartment number 22N, which he and Filbert were standing before. With a stunned expression on his face, Johnny turned to Filbert, raised one eyebrow, and asked, "Do we knock?"

Filbert chuckled and said, "Before we can even go in, I want to explain that time will move very rapidly when we are in the apartment. It will almost be as if you are watching commercials, commercials of your life. You will be seeing the life you really cannot remember because you were too young to form full memories. However, everything that happened is still inside your mind. In fact, it is what helped mold your personality. It is this time that helped make you who you are today, and these hidden memories are called paradigms."

"Par-a-die-ms", Johnny said with difficulty. "Now you've really lost me Filbert. When are you doing to program a dictionary in my mind?"

"Ha-ha Johnny - I only plant seeds. Now, I know. It is very complicated. I usually do not even share the word paradigm with most seedlings, but you are extraordinarily bright for someone your age. Think of your brain as a sponge and when you are very young you absorb everything around you even if you do not remember any of it. And those things programmed your mind. They programmed the way you think."

Johnny, now staring blankly at Filbert, jokingly said, "So Filbert, you're saying that when I was young, I resembled a type of computerized Sponge Bob?"

"Ha-ha Johnny, I am glad to see your sense of humor has returned! Let me try a different way to explain this."

"Yes, please do Filbert."

"You know what a byte of data is, right Johnny?"
"Duh, Filbert, I actually have unlimited gigabytes on my Wi-Fi at home."

"Great, and do you know a bit is smaller than a byte?"

"Yes Filbert, but why are we talking about bits and bytes?"

"Well Johnny, scientists in your world have estimated that your brain is exposed to millions and millions of bits of information a second, but your brain can only process 50 bits per second. Therefore, the rest of that information goes into your brain without you knowing it went in. Interesting right?"

"What? I don't understand that at all. How does the information go in my head if I don't know it is going in?" Johnny asked.

"Johnny, that is why I used the example of a sponge at the beginning. Just trust me on this one. It is like when you are a baby. You do not remember everything that went into your head, but it did, right? You know how to talk and walk but do you remember learning that stuff?"

"Ah, not really."

"Well, that is the idea. There is so much going on all around, every day, but most goes in unnoticed. When you are young, you have no filters and just absorb everything. Those things lead to beliefs and those are called paradigms. You can think of it as the operating system in your head."

"Uffa Filbert. Now you are telling me that when I was a child, I was Sponge Bob, Steve Jobs and Bill Gates all in one? I know I have told you many times Filbert, but it seems with each journey, things get more confusing."

Just as Filbert was about to comment, Johnny responded. "I know Filbert, seeds, patience and it will all become clear to me some day."

Filbert chuckled while Johnny looked intensely at him. Confusion was written all over Johnny's face and then he remembered the time his dad had asked him about Pete's Pub and how he knew where it was even though he hadn't studied a map of Hopewell Junction.

"Filbert, I think my dad tried to explain this to me at some point and used an example of how I know where stores are in my town even though I have never studied a map."

"Johnny, I said this before, he is a very wise man."

Johnny started to smile, and as always felt the tickle in his chest but before he could speak Filbert said, "Johnny, watch what happens inside, maybe you will understand better after you see your baby-self."

"You mean I'll be watching myself grow up?" Johnny asked very enthusiastically.

"Exactly but remember to avoid getting stuck in the details. This is even harder for adults to understand, which is why we can only show these lessons to children. Are you ready?"

"Yup."

Filbert began smiling so widely that his mouth turned into the keys of a piano. His teeth twinkled so brightly and started to play a melody that sounded like wind chimes. Then in the blink of an eye, he and Johnny were in Johnny's nursery. Johnny was stunned to be looking at his six-month-old baby-self and kept turning back to Filbert as if to ask if everything was ok. Filbert just nodded.

Johnny couldn't believe how truly beautiful the nursery was. He'd seen pictures but being there was totally different. There were tiny lights installed in the ceiling, which twinkled like stars in the night sky. In the far-right hand corner of the nursery was a very special colorful lamp. Years ago, when he and his parents were going through baby pictures, his father explained how the lamp worked. In the morning, the lamp would simulate a sunrise and at night it would replicate the colors of a sunset and the rising moon. Johnny was astonished that his parents had given so much thought to every detail of his nursery and yet he had no memory of it.

As he peered into the crib and saw his baby-self sleeping, he heard Filbert ask him, "How do you think this little baby learned all the things you know today?"

Johnny glanced at Filbert, pondered the question, and then replied, "I guess my parents and my teachers taught me."

Filbert smiled and in a slow hushed voice told Johnny, "They gave you guidance but Johnny, you taught yourself and the secret is that you learned everything by making mistakes."

Johnny stepped back a little from Filbert in disbelief but didn't say anything because he wanted to go with the flow. He wanted to see where this journey led before asking questions. He'd learned that his questions were usually answered along the way. Again, Johnny spotted Filbert's gleaming, musical smile and next they were in the living room on a sunny day. Johnny guessed it had to be sometime in the afternoon.

Before Johnny even saw his baby-self on the floor, he found himself staring out the window. He'd forgotten how much he loved the city and the great view from their apartment. They faced the west side of the city, and their building was the tallest around for many blocks. Therefore, they could see clearly above all the other buildings. From the living room window, he could see the three big bridges of the city and the huge city park. As he began moving closer to the window, he heard his baby-self cry and turned around. His mom and Cathy were seated on the sofa. He couldn't believe how young they looked.

Baby Johnny was crawling on the floor. It seemed he had hurt himself, but Johnny couldn't understand what had happened to make his baby-self cry. He noticed that his mom and Cathy were talking, but for some reason he couldn't hear their voices. He turned to Filbert and asked why he couldn't hear them. Filbert explained that their conversation would distract from the purpose of this journey.

"Johnny, their conversation isn't important to what you need to see so I pressed the mute button," he said winking at Johnny.

Johnny started watching his baby-self with much more concentration. He realized that the baby was trying desperately to stand up. He was trying to hold the side of the sofa in order to pull himself up. Each time the baby tried to stand, he fell, causing him to cry. Cathy then got on her knees next to the baby. While looking at him she pulled herself up to stand, showing baby Johnny how to pull himself up. She then sat back on the sofa. Baby Johnny just stared at Cathy and tried again and again and again, crying every time he fell.

Filbert turned to Johnny and said, "Do you see, as a baby you just try. You do not worry about appearing stupid or making mistakes. You just try and try and try."

For the third time Filbert smiled his musical smile but this time the melody was slightly different, which caused time to move forward even faster. They jumped ahead about two months and Johnny noticed his baby-self had grown a little taller.

Johnny then heard the door behind him open and felt his heart leap as his father walked through the door arriving home from work. His baby-self immediately started to giggle, pulled himself up by the side of the sofa and walked very clumsily over to his father. Mr. Prospect smiled at baby Johnny and said, "Good for you my son, I knew you could do it." Baby Johnny chuckled as he grabbed Mr. Prospect's leg. A tear formed in Johnny's eye. He turned to Filbert and asked, "Why can we hear my dad?"

Filbert explained that the positive words his father said were vital to this lesson. "Positivity, recognition of achievements, and encouragement are all very powerful Johnny," Filbert said before time jumped forward again.

In the next scene baby Johnny was sitting on the floor with his mom who held a picture book of objects. Johnny was amazed at how much time his mom had spent with him when he was a baby. He always remembered his mom working long hours at the hospital and only had memories of Cathy as the "mother" figure in his life. He thought how wrong he'd been to think that his mother cared more about her job than she did about him. He promised himself that he would recall these "commercials" often.

He watched as his mom pointed to a picture in a book and said the word "ball." He understood, due to Filbert's explanation a few moments earlier, that her words had to be important if he was able to hear the conversation. "Ball," she repeated and then he heard his baby-self say, "ah-all." Again his mom pointed to the picture, but this time she took her hand to her mouth and with her fingers she gently squeezed her lips together, more or less in the shape of a fish's mouth and slowly said, "ba, ba, bah, ba-hall, ball." Baby Johnny chuckled at her fish lips. Then it was his turn. Mrs. Prospect took her fingers and squeezed his mouth gently in the same shape that she'd done to hers causing baby Johnny to giggle before saying, "Bah."

Filbert smiled and the scene quickly changed to the city park where he and his parents would picnic on the weekends. He used to love going to the city park because there were many playgrounds, a pool, a merry-go-round, a lake and lots of trees and birds. It was such a peaceful place because the sounds of the city magically disappeared once anyone stepped a few feet into the park.

The Prospects had their favorite spot on the top of a big rock that overlooked a lake. His dad had told him before they moved out of the city that the rock had been part of the original glaciers that traveled down from the North Pole many years ago during the Ice Age. As the ice melted, the rock got dropped off in that part of the park and had been there for hundreds of millions of years. Johnny always thought of it as a special place.

Johnny noticed that baby Johnny looked about the same age as the last scene. A group of kids were playing soccer in the field next to the rock. One of the kids kicked the soccer ball too hard and it bounced near the Prospect's picnic blanket. Baby Johnny started to clap in excitement as the ball bounced passed them. Then in perfect English said, "Ball, ball, ball."

Scenes changed very quickly after that. Johnny watched his baby-self learn to drink from a cup, use a crayon, use a fork, turn on the water, flip a light switch, and even to use the toilet. He thought that so many of these things had just come naturally. He never thought that they had to be learned or "absorbed" as Filbert had told him. He watched as his baby-self made mistake after mistake yet continued trying until he learned each new thing.

Next Filbert and Johnny were in the kitchen. Johnny noticed that his "baby-self" was now a toddler, taller and probably about three-and-a-half years old in this scene. It was probably right before they moved out of the city. Toddler Johnny was standing on his stool next to Cathy watching her get ready to cook dinner. Suddenly Johnny grabbed the first finger on his right hand. It was throbbing with so much pain, which made him remember exactly what was going to happen in this scene.

Cathy told toddler Johnny he had to come down from the step stool and sit at the table because she was about to turn on the stove. She explained that it was too hot for little children. Toddler Johnny did as he was told. She then turned on the stove and walked over to the refrigerator to get the meat. Johnny wished he could've reached out to stop his younger self, but as soon as Cathy turned her back, toddler Johnny ran over to the stool and stuck his finger out to touch the flame. He screamed so loudly causing Cathy to drop the meat and eggs on the floor as she ran to his aid.

Toddler Johnny was screaming in pain from the burn. Cathy carried him over to the freezer, grabbed some ice and put it on his finger. She then focused on toddler Johnny with puppy dog eyes and said to him, "Trust me Johnny, everything is ok. Play a game with me. Ok? Please."

Toddler Johnny continued sobbing but couldn't take his eyes off Cathy and said, "Ok" in the saddest, smallest voice.

"Let's play peak-a-boo. Ok Johnny?"

Toddler Johnny just gazed at her while Johnny was astonished at how calm Cathy behaved, and how calming her actions were. For a brief moment he saw a purple light shine from the center of Cathy's chest. He rapidly glanced over at Filbert but then quickly turned back afraid to miss something because all he remembered was that he burned himself.

"I'm going to count to three," Cathy said, "and then when I say peek-a-boo, we'll look at your finger, ok Johnny?"

"Hurt," toddler Johnny said in a whimpering voice.

Cathy kissed toddler Johnny on the forehead and said, "I know Johnny, but because you're scared, it makes the hurt worse. Once we take a look, I'm sure you'll start feeling better. That's always the way it is Johnny. The things we don't know, the things in the dark always seem the scariest but we have to look to start to make everything all better. Play with me, ok?"

Johnny again swiftly glanced over at Filbert, who smiled at Johnny with one eyebrow raised. Toddler Johnny said whimpering, "Ok."

"1-2-3, peek-a-boo," Cathy sang in a very cheerful sounding voice.

They both looked. The finger was red, but not blistered. Cathy had caught it in time with the ice. She then held toddler Johnny's face with both hands, staring into his eyes and said, "It will all be ok."

"Ouch," toddler Johnny mumbled to Cathy.

Cathy then said something else that Johnny hadn't remembered but as soon she started saying it, he also started reciting it with her, word for word, which sent chills down his back.

"Pain is only your body's way of reminding you that you learned a valuable lesson not to touch fire. That's all this is," Cathy continued. "It's an opportunity to learn something Johnny. It isn't anything to be afraid of. Trust me Johnny. I'll never lie to you. You now learned not to touch fire, right?"

"Right," toddler Johnny said in an enraged voice.

"Well then," Cathy said, "I think we should have some ice cream and celebrate that you learned something new."

POP! Johnny and Filbert were back in the white room. Johnny realized he was still holding his finger, surprised a memory could actually cause his finger to throb with pain.

"Filbert."

"Yes, Johnny."

"I have lots of questions."

"I would hope so" Filbert responded while raising both eyebrows. "You need to ask questions to learn. I think I may have told you that once before," Filbert said while chuckling right before turning into a blinking question mark.

"Boy, you are a jokester, aren't you Filbert?" Johnny said while laughing hysterically.

"Life and learning should always be approached with fun Johnny. Why shouldn't we have fun with everything in life? Wouldn't you agree?

"I am learning to, my little chubby friend."

Filbert began bouncing off the walls like a tennis ball and they both started laughing uncontrollably until Filbert said, "So what do you want to ask first?"
Johnny, as he usually found himself at some point while with Filbert, held his stomach from laughing so hard. When he stopped laughing, he sat down crossed legged on the floor and said, "First Filbert, Cathy spoke to the baby me with big words. How's it possible I understood them?"

"Great question Johnny!" Filbert said enthusiastically. "You did not understand the words, but you understood the emotion in those words. You understood that you were safe. How do you think you learned words before school? You learned the feelings of the words first. It' why I use big words with you as well. Remember, seeds, Silly Putty, stretching. Does that make sense?"

"Yeah, it makes sense enough, I guess. Another thing Filbert, I noticed a purple light come from Cathy when she was trying to calm me down. Well, I mean toddler me, after burning myself. What did that mean?"

Filbert again explained to Johnny that imagination is fueled by love. And that love and imagination are so similar, and so connected to each other, that at that moment Cathy was completely connected to her love for him. She was so connected to her love to protect him and make him better, that she glowed.

"It was her connection to taking care of you and her love for you in that moment that caused her to glow."

For the first time, Johnny clearly understood how strongly his family loved him.

"What else do you want to ask me Johnny?"

"Why, as a child, did I not seem to get upset when I made a mistake. Why?"
"That is a great question Johnny, as that was precisely what I wanted you to get from this journey," Filbert said in the most joyful tone. Filbert went on to explain that it is only when people start growing up that they learn to label things as mistakes.

"See Johnny," Filbert started, "remember how we talked about being careful with words and the energy words can have?"

"Yes, I seem to remember something about that," Johnny said jokingly.

"Well, when you were that young, you were surrounded by encouraging energy, encouraging words. You were not aware of the word 'mistake.' You were not aware of anything but trying, trying, trying and trying. You had not learned to fear and judge things in your life. It is only when people get older that they start to worry about what other people will think and say. They start to worry about being right and fearing mistakes instead of being open to learning and to trying."

Filbert continued, "You see how you made so many of what you now call 'mistakes,' but without them you would have never learned to stand, walk and even speak. Without them you would not really have learned anything. Do you see now that the word mistake is negative? Do you see that mistake just means more practice is needed? That it means the opportunity to grow and learn is still there? Most of the time people are afraid of mistakes because they do not want to look stupid. Remember how fear removed you from your imagination. How can you grow and truly learn without imagination - without mistakes?"

Johnny absent-mindedly glanced at Filbert. He was thinking about everything Filbert had said. There was so much to take in. Yet, it felt so weird to him not to worry about making mistakes. He could fail at school, he could get hurt, and there were so many things that could happen by getting something wrong.

"Filbert," Johnny began in a very humbled voice, "I really don't get what you are saying. I understand the idea that it means more practice, but I could fail school with too many mistakes or hurt myself if I make a mistake riding my bike, so how are they a good thing?"

Filbert stroked his chin with his tiny little hand as he'd done earlier and finally said to Johnny, "Remember we talked about how in the Pimby world words have different meanings than in your world, such as when you freaked out about the word test during one of our first meetings?"

Johnny nodded his head, signaling he remembered.

"Again," Filbert continued, "the same thing is happening now. I am not saying that what you just explained to me is not true. What I am saying is the word 'mistake' holds so much pressure, so much negativity. I am also saying that you need them to grow and learn and that your worrying about making mistakes stops your growth."

"Think of it this way, in the past you would get upset and feel stupid and embarrassed when you made a mistake. I am just suggesting that there is no reason to feel bad because a mistake is a natural way for you to understand that you need more practice. Do not define it as you are stupid or a failure, instead define it as you are still learning, still growing. Define it as a period of 'not yet.' Maybe try thinking, the next time you make what you call a 'mistake' in your world, *isn't that interesting, back to the drawing board.* You can only ever do your best Johnny, and if you approach everything in life with the intention of doing your best, you will then approach everything from positivity and imagination will flow. I am not saying to be careless. All I am saying is to stop worrying and approach it differently. Worry creates fear Johnny. Fear is a good tool to protect you from danger. Worry is not real danger, but the more you worry the more you make it into danger. Understand?"

"Not really Filbert. I am trying, but it is not clicking."

"Hmm, ok Johnny let me explain it another way. Think about this because I know you like baseball. The best pitchers in baseball threw a lot of wrong pitches at the beginning. The difference is they did not dwell on 'mistakes.' They focused on needing more practice. Do you know who Babe Ruth was?"

"Yeah, I do Filbert. He was one of the best baseball players in history. He is famous for being one of the best home run hitters ever."

"Johnny, you really are amazing with all the facts you know, but do you want to know something else amazing about Babe Ruth?"

"For sure Filbert!"

"He was known as the King of Strikeouts. He struck out over 1300 times in his career."

"Really Filbert?"

"Yes Johnny. He is famous for saying 'Every strike brings me closer to the next home run,' and 'Never let the fear of striking out keep you from coming up to bat.'" In other words, don't let fear of mistakes stop you."

"That is incredible Filbert. Thanks for telling me that. I am going to paste a picture of him on my bulletin board above my desk to remind me to always go to bat."

"Great idea Johnny! Oh, and one other thing. You say in your world 'practice makes perfect,' but I want you to trust me that there is no perfect. Practice brings improvement, practice brings progress, but nothing can ever be perfect."

Filbert went on to explain that it may be a long time before Johnny could completely understand this lesson and that once again it was like a seed being planted that hopefully will grow in the future.

"Johnny, it will be the experiences in your life that will help you fully understand all of what I have been trying to show you during our journeys," Filbert said while staring at him intensely. "All of what I am showing you is like a treasure map for you to follow or not. These are ideas that you will come to understand more deeply if you stay connected."

"Ok."

"Johnny, I want to give you some homework."

"Oh no way - not you too! My mom already has me doing homework during the summer."

"I know Johnny, but the exercises I want you to do are a bit different than traditional homework."

"Uffa, homework is homework Filbert," Johnny said with frustration.

"Johnny, trust me, I would never ask you to do anything if I did not believe it would benefit you."
"Yeah, I know. So, what do I have to do?"

"First, I want you to have a cup of T.E.A. every day."

"What? Filbert, I think you're going bonkers," Johnny said laughingly. "How is that homework? And I don't even like tea."

"Ha Johnny, I got you! I do not mean tea as in the drink. I am using the acronym T.E.A. to help you remember."

"Filbert, what is an acronym?"

"Johnny, remember how the name ROY G BIV helped you recall all the colors of light?"

"Yeah, why?"

"Well ROY G BIV is an acronym for all those colors. When I said I want you to have a cup of T.E.A. every day it is because I want you to remember three important things on a daily basis: your Thoughts, your Efforts, and your Actions. You can only ever control these three things in your life. So remember to focus your thoughts on the positive, make sure your effort is always to do your best and that your actions are constructive."

"Ok, that's easy. So, you want me to think about my thoughts, efforts, and actions every day."

"Yes Johnny, but there is something else I want you to do as well."

"I knew it sounded too easy," Johnny said frustratedly.

"Johnny, you should know by now to keep your mind open. Your frustration is coming from your expectations that what I am going to ask you to do will be something hard, or it will be something you do not like. Maybe it would be better to stay curious and not worry about what it might be. What do you think about that?"

"You're right, ok, so what's the other little gem you have for me as homework," Johnny said sarcastically.

"Well, that is a slightly better attitude," Filbert replied sarcastically before continuing. "Each night before you go to bed, I want you to recount only and all those things that you did correctly and that were fun experiences during the day, ok?"

"That's it? That's all my homework?"

"Yes Johnny. By the way, did you know that your favorite Roman Emperor Marcus Aurelius practiced something very similar?"

"Really, that's so cool, I had no idea."

"Any other questions Johnny because our time on this journey is coming to an end?"

"Yeah," Johnny said. "Cathy used your words almost exactly when she told me not to be afraid and that she would never lie to me when I burned myself as a toddler. I can't help but wonder about the similarity. Did you notice she talked like you?"

Filbert's eye twinkled and in a very mysterious voice he said, "So she did Johnny. So she did."

Johnny woke in his bed at about 8 a.m. with the warmth of the sun on his face. It was a beautiful morning and he felt so excited about all the opportunities the day held for him to learn and grow. As he stretched in his bed, he noticed that the sun filtering through his window seemed to spell something on his ceiling. As he looked closely, he read the words: Never stop trying - let imagination flow!

Johnny then heard the jingling of his mom's keys, which meant she was getting ready to leave for work. He quickly jumped out of bed, ran down the stairs and gave her a hug.

His mom focused on him with a curious look on her face and asked, "What brought that on Johnny?"

Johnny told her he had a dream about how they used to spend a lot of time together when he was a baby. They both smiled.

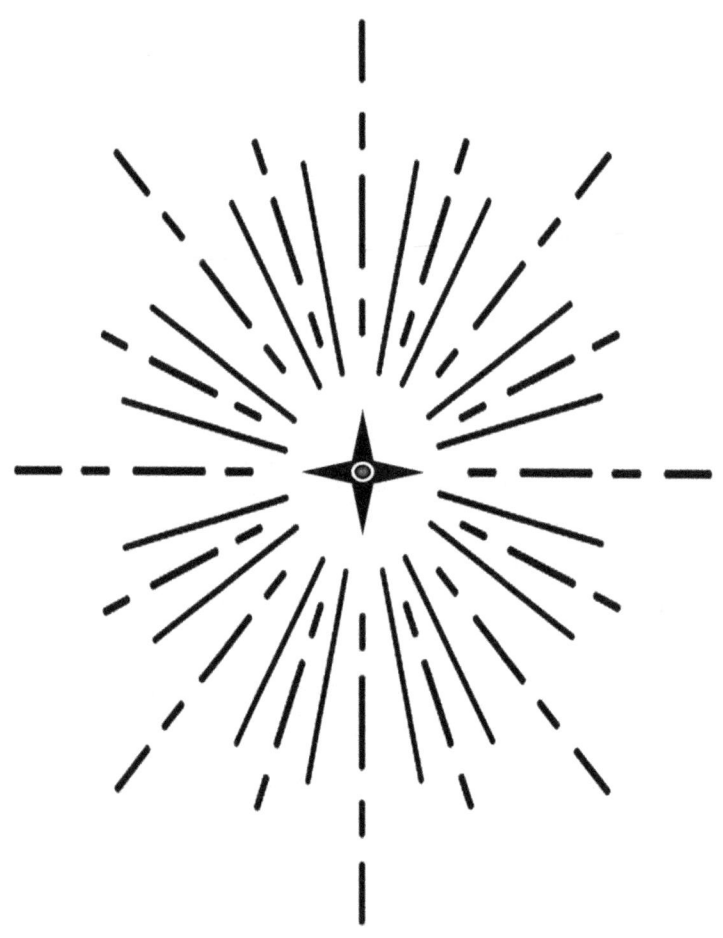

Filbert's Gift

Johnny was awestruck with all that had happened since meeting Filbert. He knew that their time together was coming to an end as his birthday was quickly approaching. It seemed impossible that it had already been almost nine weeks since they'd first met.

Hmm, magical number nine, just like Filbert mentioned to me during one of our first conversations, how funny, he thought to himself.

He tried to recall everything but there was just so much. First off, he now had his own golden temple. He learned the importance of being respectful of nature, of people and to respect himself. He learned to be careful with his words, to be positive, to always try and focus on doing his best. He remembered floating above the city and floating out to the Sun where he learned that everything is connected. He also learned that the sound of the Sun is also the sound of the creative engine.

Johnny had so many images flashing through his mind as he watched the little smiling faces in the raindrops falling past the windows. He finally remembered how Filbert told him that everything has its own nature and when you accept your true nature you are the happiest.

I guess my true nature is to let imagination flow and be positive because that is when I am the happiest.

He then started thinking about a more dramatic event that occurred a few nights ago while he was camping in Mickey's backyard. Mickey had stopped by and asked Johnny what was going on with him because Johnny always wanted to be alone. Johnny explained that he just had a lot on his mind. He didn't want to make up a story or lie to Mickey to cover up the truth that he'd been thinking about Filbert, so he told him a truthful but short answer.

Mickey accepted his answer and then grabbed Johnny by the shoulders and shook him roughly while saying, "Get over it man. You need something to take your mind off whatever is bothering you and that means you are coming over tomorrow night and we are camping in the backyard."

Camping in each other's backyards was a ritual they started pretty much after they first met years ago. The thought of camping with Mickey made Johnny super happy. As Johnny smiled, he felt a warm tickling sensation in his chest, which he now knew meant his orange light was shining. He quickly glanced down at his chest out of habit, which prompted Mickey to ask, "Dude, what are you doing now?"

"Oh nothing. I felt something strange and thought it might ruin my shirt."

"Johnny, your mom has you too worried about your clothes. Wear some old clothes tomorrow when you come over to camp. That way you don't have to worry about getting them dirty," Mickey said with a smirk on his face. "Deal?"

"Deal!"

Johnny loved to camp in Mickey's backyard. Johnny and his dad used to camp a lot when they lived in Clear City, either on the roof of their apartment or in the city park. He missed it, which was one of the many reasons he liked camping in Mickey's backyard. The other reason was Mickey's mom would bake the most delicious brownies and cupcakes. Camping in Hopewell Junction was also much more fun because there were fewer streetlights than in the city, which let Johnny see many more stars. At that moment he remembered again how Cathy once told him that her grandmother said everything is made of stardust. That memory always made him smile.

Johnny arrived the next night about 6 p.m. and Mr. Dakota already had hamburgers and hotdogs grilling on the barbeque. As soon as Mr. Dakota saw Johnny, he said his usual greeting, "Hi Son."

"Hi Mr. D," said Johnny. "The food smells so good. I could smell it when I walked across the street. I hoped you were going to make your famous blue cheese stuffed burgers."

"I'm making them just for you Johnny. Tell me, how's everything been going with you? I don't see you over here as much anymore," Mr. Dakota said with the slight sound of worry in his voice.

"Yeah, I know, but all is good. It's just I've got a lot going on and my mom has me studying like crazy."

"Well Johnny, never forget to keep time for fun. It's incredibly important to enjoy life."

Johnny noticed that right after Mr. Dakota finished the sentence, a yellow light started to glow in the middle of his chest. Johnny felt so special not only because he could see it but also because he knew it was a sign that Mr. Dakota really cared for him and believed deep in his heart that it was important for Johnny to enjoy life.

As the night went on, Johnny witnessed the colored light of both Mr. and Mrs. Dakota. Mrs. Dakota had a deep green light. Mickey's oldest brother Billy had a light blue light. His sister Suzie's light was neon pink and Tommy had a Ferrari red light.

173

Johnny laughed to himself at how the entire backyard was flickering with different colored lights shining from everyone, which brought to mind being with Filbert in the sunflower field. About 9:30 p.m. Mickey's parents went inside while Johnny and Mickey continued to lay on the grass in front of the tent gazing up at the sky. Mickey then asked Johnny, "Has the Pimby ever come back?"

"What Mickey? What do you mean?" Johnny asked in a nervous voice.

"Well, the last time we had a sleepover was the night when we were searching for the Pimby and you sleeping over tonight reminded me of it. We haven't really spoken much in a long time, so I was wondering if one of the things on your mind is the Pimby."

"Honestly, Mickey, I have been thinking about the world of Pimbies a lot lately, but for tonight let's talk about something else."

"Ok Johnny. Your call."

As the night went on, the two of them talked about movies, video games, and the new girl that moved in a few blocks away who they had seen riding her bicycle, the same girl Johnny was staring at the day he fell off his skateboard into the bushes. He told Mickey about it and they started laughing so loudly the tent started to shake. Johnny thought about how he should've laughed like this when he'd fallen instead of getting so embarrassed and feeling stupid. They, of course, also talked about school starting soon.

It was a perfectly dark night and the stars shone brighter than ever. As Johnny was staring at the stars, he said hello to them in his mind. Just then Johnny and Mickey both saw a shooting star. Mickey quickly blurt out, "We have to make a wish!"

Johnny did make a wish but had noticed something rather strange about the shooting star. To him it resembled a little waving hand and not truly a star. He'd learned over the last few visits with Filbert that many more things were possible than he ever thought.

Johnny again remembered how his dad had once explained to him that human brains can only process a fraction of the information going on in the world and if one just expands the way they think about things, they could notice much more.

Huh, that's exactly what Filbert tried to explain to me when he talked about bits and bytes. I wonder why my dad has told me so many things similar to what Filbert tells me?

He remembered his dad once used an example of how a dog knows its owner is coming home minutes before the person shows up. "They can sense the energy," he'd told him using it as an example of what he meant about how humans don't notice all that goes on around them.

"The goal in life is to always expand, grow and learn," Johnny only now recalled him saying.

Johnny also remembered how his dad had once told him that for hundreds of years birds have followed the same migration paths and some say it is because the birds leave a trail of energy that acts like a highway for the next generation of birds to follow. As he recalled these conversations, he became convinced, more than ever, that his father truly knew about Pimbies because he always talked a lot about energy and imagination.

Johnny then thought to himself that he would try an experiment. In his mind he imagined saying hello again to the stars.

Mickey was walking around the yard with his neck bent back continuing to look for more shooting stars. Johnny then gazed up at the sky, saying hello to the stars once again in his mind and swoosh…another shooting star.

"Johnny, did you see that? Another one! Boy, we are lucky tonight! Make another wish!" Mickey said with tremendous excitement.

Johnny knew, without a shadow of a doubt, that somehow his greeting the stars were causing them to shoot. He did it one more time and once again another star shot across the night sky. Mickey was so consumed with searching for shooting stars that Johnny took the opportunity to close his eyes and - poof - he instantly found himself at the golden temple. He immediately glimpsed up at the ceiling and remembered how the stars twinkled more when he smiled at them. This time he said out loud, "Hello stars," and immediately the stars all started to sway back and forth as if they were waving hello. He knew that was what was happening now with Mickey.

When he opened his eyes, worry grabbed hold of him because he thought Mickey might have caught him with his eyes closed, but when he checked his watch, he saw not even a whole second had passed. *I can't believe I was worried,* he thought to himself, *Filbert had told me not to be.*

The next morning Johnny woke up before Mickey because he heard what sounded like something squeaking. He walked out of the tent and peered out towards the horizon in the direction of the sound, yet all he noticed was the first light of the morning sun rising over the mountains. As the light grew brighter, the squeaking sound grew louder. He then realized he was literally hearing the sunlight extend over the mountains. Johnny then stretched out his arms, let out a big yawn and smiled. He felt so thankful for all the things that were happening in his life.

As he climbed back into the tent Mickey started waking up. As Mickey turned in Johnny's direction, an orange feather with green zebra stripes landed on Mickey's nose. Mickey sneezed and picked up the feather. He twirled it between his fingers for a second and then said to Johnny, "Hey this is the same feather we found in your room when we had the pillow fight. You saved it?"

Johnny looked at Mickey unsure about how to answer him.

"That's so weird Mickey," Johnny said in a drawn-out voice. "No, I didn't save the feather, but how weird that you found it on your nose."

"Yeah, right," Mickey said. "Lame prank if you ask me! Let's go inside and see what my mom is making for breakfast."

Johnny was overjoyed about Filbert's impending visit, which of course made his chest tickle. It then occurred to him that this was probably their last visit together because tomorrow he would turn nine. Just then, he sensed the warmth in his chest going away and as expected, when he looked down, he indeed did see the light start to fade.

Why should I be unhappy? Filbert is visiting soon. That's what I should focus on instead of it being the last time. With that thought his light shone across the room.

Breakfast was delicious. Johnny always loved eating breakfast at Mickey's house because his parents cooked sausage, bacon, homemade biscuits, and pancakes whenever he slept over, all the stuff his mom would never allow him to eat in his house. This breakfast was extra special because Mrs. Dakota used food coloring to make a smiley face in Johnny's pancake as an early birthday celebration.

"It seems you boys are growing up so fast," Mrs. Dakota said. "I remember when you first moved into the neighborhood, Johnny, but of course how could I forget with our son stealing your boxes and dragging them over to our house to make a fort or playhouse or whatever you boys wound up calling it. Even then we could tell you were a wonderful boy. I also remember how the sky was colored a deep orange that day. It was such a strange sunset that I have never forgotten it." Mrs. Dakota had her hand over her heart when she talked about the orange sky.

Johnny stared at Mrs. Dakota very intently for a moment or two and noticed her light was very bright and wondered if the orange sky had a special meaning. *Maybe I will ask Filbert,* Johnny thought to himself. *Nah, I don't need to know the answer to everything.* Finally -- Johnny started going with the flow.

He headed back over to his house later that afternoon and could smell a cake in the oven. He heard Cathy singing a song and caught her skipping across the floor when he walked into the kitchen. For a moment she appeared to be about 12 years old.

"Oh Johnny," she said, "I didn't hear you come in, but I'm glad you are here. I made an extra special cookie crumb icing for your cake. Do you want to lick the beaters?"

Johnny didn't even answer her before grabbing the beaters. Within seconds his face was covered in icing.

"Didn't they feed you over there?" Cathy joked.

"Cathy, do you know what time my parents are coming home tonight?" Johnny asked before turning back to lick the remaining icing off the beaters.

"I know your father has to stay in the city and I'm not sure when your mom will be home, but she did tell me she will be taking you into the city tomorrow for a birthday breakfast. She told me the three of you will spend the day in the park. Unfortunately, she didn't mention what time she'll be home tonight, but I am sure it will be after dinner. I hope that doesn't upset you," Cathy said with a little concern in her voice.

"Oh, not at all" Johnny replied. He realized he was learning that he had the choice to feel happy or sad in any occasion and, while he could feel sad about his dad having to stay in the city, there was no reason to be upset or disappointed because that would mean he had expectations. He'd learned so much from Filbert and knew he had so many things to celebrate. *Go with the flow,* he thought to himself.

After dinner, Johnny went to his room and grabbed a new notebook from his desk. He decided to write down everything that happened over these past nine weeks. Johnny had never kept a journal, but he wanted to do everything in his power to never forget Filbert's visits, what Filbert looked like, and all the quotes and lessons Filbert had taught him. The hours flew by and even though Johnny's hand would cramp at times, he did not want to stop writing.

A little after 10 p.m. his mom knocked on his door.

"Come in," Johnny said in a distracted voice.

As Johnny's mom walked in, he observed there was something quite different about her. She wasn't thinner, but she appeared lighter. As a matter of fact, the more he thought about it, the more she seemed to float across the room. She usually would walk very heavy footed and fast, but now she was walking so gracefully, almost as if she were a ballet dancer.

"Johnny, what are you still doing up? I saw your light was on and while I know you're going to be nine in two hours, it doesn't mean you can stay awake past 10 p.m., especially since we're leaving for the city early tomorrow to meet your father."

Johnny grasped even the tone of his mom's voice had changed. It was much softer, and she spoke more slowly. Not that she had a mean voice, but she would usually talk as if she were giving orders.

"I know Mom. I just wanted to write some things down." Soon after Johnny said those words, he wished he could've taken them back. He knew he wasn't supposed to share information about Filbert's visits and became concerned his mother would want to take a look at his journal.

"You're not doing schoolwork, are you Johnny?"

Johnny honestly explained to her that he had decided to start a journal. She tilted her head to the side, smiled, and said, "Johnny you really are growing into a fine man."

She patted and kissed his head before leaving the room. Approaching the door, she asked him to not stay up too late because his ninth birthday is so special, and she did not want him to be tired. As the door shut, Johnny could see her pink light shining in the hallway.

She had never mentioned his ninth birthday being special before. It had always been his father that made a big deal about it. Now Johnny was sure there was something very different about his mother. He decided he would ask Filbert about his mom. He knew he could go to the temple, but he also wanted to continue writing. He turned off the big lamp in his room and kept the small lamp on his desk on while he wrote quickly.

Johnny was glancing down at his journal, finally taking a break from writing to give his hand a needed rest. Suddenly, he observed the words begin to float on the page like alphabet cereal in a bowl of milk. As he reached out to touch them, he fell through the page and was zigging and zagging through what felt like a huge water park slide finally landing in the white room.

"I wanted your final entrance to be a splash!" Filbert bellowed, laughing and twirling around the room.

"That was a fun way to come to visit you Filbert," Johnny said with a huge grin on his face, "You should've done that earlier. I've always been a fan of amusement park type rides."

Johnny and Filbert usually spoke first before the room would vibrate and change into their journey, but this time the room started to swirl with more colors than Johnny had ever seen. It reminded him of a huge Fourth of July fireworks show. All the colors sparkled as if they were diamonds and drops of what looked like paint started falling from the ceiling. It took some time for Johnny to clearly focus on the hundreds upon hundreds of drops. But as he did, he recognized that they were all different types of Pimbies. Pimbies of all shapes and sizes as far as the eye could see surrounded him. In fact, he felt as if he were in a huge field of colored marbles, because the Pimbies in the distance looked like bright colored balls.

While staring at all the Pimbies, he began to hear what sounded like a roar coming towards him. It had started from far in the back and grew louder and louder until the wave of sound finally hit him causing him to fall backwards by the sheer force of the wind that carried the words HAPPY BIRTHDAY JOHNNY!

When he stood back up all the other Pimbies were gone.

"Where did they all go Filbert? I really didn't even get a chance to look at all of them," Johnny said in a flustered voice.

"Johnny, they can only come for a moment. They are other people's Pimbies, and it is only for a ninth birthday greeting that they can present themselves to a person who is not their seedling. Pimbies are able to multiply in order to be in many places at once to say, 'Happy Birthday.' But once we have said 'Happy Birthday,' we all must return to our own seedlings."

"Well, that was so great. This is the best way to start a birthday!" Johnny said at the top of his voice.

"So, you are not sad that it is the last time we will see each other, Johnny?"

"Filbert, I am, I'm very sad, but I've learned not to let the negative take away from the fun I am having now."

"Great, Johnny. You have really grown over these last nine weeks. I am incredibly happy to have been your Pimby. I am very thankful that we got to meet."

"Me too Filbert. So, where are we going today? What are we going to do on this journey?" Johnny asked impatiently.

"Actually Johnny, your last visit, your last lesson requires no travel, no journey. We just stay here because the only thing left to do is give you a gift. You've already turned nine. The rest is up to you." Filbert said in a very fatherly voice.

Johnny started to fantasize about all the different things the gift might be. He thought of everything from a magic wand to a time capsule, to gold and precious gems. He went on and on with his fantasies of what it could be and suddenly remembered the game show with the guy who was disappointed because the car he won wasn't the color he wanted. This caused Johnny to realize he was closing himself off, so he let go of his expectations and decided to just go with the flow.

Filbert smiled at Johnny as if he were able to read his mind and knew Johnny had let go of his expectations. Filbert shocked Johnny when he explained that the ninth birthday was so magical that only in this space for a short time can a Pimby actually see inside their seedling's mind.

"It is our way to see if the seeds we planted have taken root."

"Have they?" Johnny asked.

"Unfortunately, Johnny, I can't tell you, you know the rules and all."

He then went on to tell Johnny that he had seen that Johnny was wondering what the gift might be and how he then let go of the expectation and chose to let it be a surprise.

"I am very proud of you Johnny."

Johnny smiled back but also felt a little weird that Filbert could read his mind. Filbert was quick to explain that he couldn't truly read his thoughts, but that Johnny's thought process was like a slide show Filbert was able to watch.

"Again Johnny, it is just our way to see how much you have learned," were Filbert's final words before pulling the tiniest gold box Johnny had ever seen out from under his fur and handing it to Johnny.

Johnny stared at the box. He held it so delicately being afraid to break it or drop it. It was so tiny. He then looked at Filbert with bewilderment.

"Filbert, but this box is an exact miniature of the room in the middle of my temple, right down to the two doors I've never opened."

"I know Johnny, now when you open these small doors you will also be opening the big doors at your temple. They are one in the same. Open it," Filbert whispered in the most persuading voice.

A shimmering silver light burst from the box as soon as Johnny opened it. As he peeked inside, he saw a tiny piece of sand. The light coming from the grain of sand shone so intensely that Johnny couldn't keep looking at it and just as he was about to close the box Filbert said, "Take it out."

"But what is it Filbert?"

"It is a key, Johnny. Honestly, it is more than a key, it is a piece of imagination. It is a piece of our world, of this white room, of anything and everything. It is energy."

Johnny was awestruck to be holding a piece of imagination, a piece of energy. He took it out slowly, held it in the palm of his hand and stared at it. He turned to Filbert and said, "I don't know what to say. THANK YOU, THANK YOU FROM THE BOTTOM OF MY HEART!"

Just then the grain of sand rose from Johnny's palm into the air. Johnny watched in amazement as the grain of sand started to spin faster and faster. Johnny immediately recognized the humming sound made by the spinning action. It was the same humming sound he used to hear before Filbert would visit - the same sound as the sun. Then without warning the grain of sand shot at Johnny, right into his chest, piercing his heart. Johnny fell back, unconscious.

Happy Birthday

Johnny woke up a little before 6 a.m. He immediately grabbed his chest. He was fine.

Was this all a dream, he thought to himself. Why didn't Filbert say goodbye and what was with the grain of sand?

So many questions were running through his mind. Then he remembered the journal he'd started last night about all the adventures with Filbert. He went over to his desk and gasped when he saw the journal was blank.

"I don't understand," he said out loud, throwing the journal onto the floor.

Just then, as if a wind were blowing through the room, the pages of the journal started to turn. Johnny ran over to the journal and picked it up. Written on the first page that blew open were the words BE FLEXIBLE. The wind came again and scrawled across the second page that blew open were the words LET IT FLOW.

"Psst…Psst."

Johnny twirled around the room after hearing that sound. It was one of the first sounds he heard when he first met Filbert, but Filbert was nowhere to be found. Johnny fought hard against becoming discouraged or angry, but he was confused at everything happening. Just then Johnny's closet door opened. As Johnny walked over to the closet, he saw his reflection in the long mirror on the inside of the closet door. He paused for a minute. He couldn't believe what he saw, but quickly remembered the words BE FLEXIBLE.

Johnny's reflection was pulsating. His entire body looked like it had a layer of diamond-like shimmering dust around it, pulsing bigger and smaller, almost as if it were breathing. Then he noticed his orange light was so bright and in the center of it was a shimmering silver grain of sand.

Wow, that is what Filbert meant when we first met. That is what he meant when he said we were connected in ways I could not have understood at the beginning. He, his lessons, the POSSIBILITIES, IMAGINATION, and MAGIC are all part of me. I just had to BELIEVE and when I truly believed it all, it all became part of me. He became part of me forever, Johnny thought to himself.

"Psst…Psst," Johnny heard again.

He closed his eyes and went to his golden temple and arrived in front of the two large golden doors to the secret inner sanctuary. He wasn't at all surprised that upon opening the doors Filbert was waiting for him in an entirely white room. Filbert didn't speak and didn't have to. Johnny understood that by Filbert giving him a piece of his world, he'd actually given him a piece of himself, which meant that Filbert would always be with him.

Johnny opened his eyes, and the wind blew through his room again, turning the pages of his journal. On the ninth page in the journal were these words: THE KEY IS TO ALWAYS BE THANKFUL. "THANK YOU" ARE THE TWO MOST POWERFUL WORDS IN THE UNIVERSE.

Johnny sat with the journal open thinking about those words. He then counted that there were eighteen words, and not only were they on the ninth page, but the ninth line of the ninth page. He felt so special at having been given the gift to see the world so differently. It was just as Filbert promised when he originally asked Johnny's permission to change the way he saw the world.

Johnny closed the journal and put it on his desk. He glanced out his window, opened the screen, stuck his head out and gave thanks for everything in his life: his friends, his family, the blue sky, the baby birds singing in the tree outside his window, and of course Filbert. He realized that the greatest gift is to notice the gifts you already have and to be thankful for them. Immediately after saying "Thank you," Johnny watched everything shimmer for a moment, as far as he could see. In addition, it also seemed like the entire world took a deep breath in that moment, expanding for a split second and then returning to normal.

Cool, he thought to himself. Johnny then made a profound commitment to himself to say "thank you" every morning when he first woke up.

There were many life lessons Johnny had learned from Filbert - many he still did not fully understand but trusted he would as he got older. After making a commitment to say, "thank you" to himself every morning, Johnny remembered Filbert explaining that being careful with your words did not only mean being careful about saying negative things. Filbert had once told him, "Johnny one of the best ways to respect yourself and be careful with your words is to only make commitments you are willing to keep."

Filbert had told Johnny that when people make a commitment and then don't keep it, it feels like using words such as, I'm a failure, I lied to myself, I can't do this or that, because the action of making a commitment and then ignoring it is a very negative action. It is a type of self-betrayal.

Johnny recalled Filbert's words, "It is not only our words that we have to be careful with, but also our actions. Think of a cup of T.E.A. Johnny, to help you remember that you only have control over your Thoughts, Efforts and Actions."

While he was closing the screen to the window, his mom knocked on the door.

"Come in," he said.

"Happy Birthday, my son," she said, and he noticed she was crying.

"Mom, why are you crying?" Johnny asked.

"Because Johnny, you're growing into a fine young man and I'm so thankful you're my son."

They hugged and then he said, "Mom, you seem different these last few days. Is everything ok?"

"Oh Johnny, everything is very ok. I just feel so much happier. It's as if the energy in the house has changed. Everything just seems brighter. I don't know if that makes sense to you, Johnny. Does it?"

"Yes, Mom, it makes a lot of sense," Johnny replied with a big smile on his face and a glow in his chest, while his mom's pink light shone brighter.

His mom then told him he had to get ready to go to the city. She left the room and Johnny quickly showered and got dressed. He went to his mirror one more time and not only was his body still pulsing with the power of imagination but the diamond-like shimmering dust was now changing into all the colors of the rainbow just like Filbert had when they first met. Johnny smiled and once again said, "thank you."

"So, Johnny," began his mom, "let me tell you the schedule of your birthday festivities."

Mrs. Prospect explained to Johnny that they were going to have breakfast in his father's office building and later in the day go for a picnic in the park, finishing with dinner at an outdoor café and ice cream at Frosty's. Johnny was thrilled about the plans for his birthday and about going back to the city, especially after having just visited it with Filbert during their journey of memories. The journey to his old apartment with Filbert reminded him of how much he truly loved the city, all the people, noise and even the traffic.

Mr. Prospect worked in one of the tallest buildings almost exactly in the middle of the city. Johnny had not visited his office since his father's big promotion party a few years ago. Johnny remembered the party had taken place in a special, big round room with ceiling to floor windows and a glass dome ceiling. The room, called the Cloud Club, was on the top of the building and had a 360-degree view of the city.

As soon as the taxi dropped Johnny and his mom at his father's office, Johnny thought about how Mickey hadn't stopped by in the morning to wish him a happy birthday.

I guess we did leave super early, he thought to himself, remembering Mickey liked to sleep.

After walking through the revolving doors leading to the lobby, Johnny saw the brightest electric blue light coming from the direction of the elevators. He immediately ran toward the light knowing that it was his father waiting out of sight near the elevators. The security guard yelled at him to stop and get a pass, but Johnny just ran past and jumped towards his dad's open arms. They hugged for what felt like an exceptionally long time.

"Happy Birthday, my Son. How was the train?"

"Great, Dad. I miss taking the train. It's so much fun!"

"Yeah, it's a great way to travel. You can just sit back and let your imagination flow," Mr. Prospect said with a grin on his face.

"Exactly!" Johnny said with a matching grin on his face.

When they all got into the elevator, Mr. Prospect pressed the button marked "CC," which Johnny knew meant the Cloud Club.

"Dad," Johnny said, "I thought no one is allowed to use the Cloud Club for family. I thought it was only for clients and business events."

"That's true Johnny, but when I told my partners about your ninth birthday, they insisted we use the club because they also believe that the ninth birthday is super special."

"It's already been the best birthday ever!" Johnny said so warmly before holding both his parents' hands and saying, "Thank you."

The door to the Cloud Club had a special electronic keypad lock, similar to that of an ATM machine. It was a video screen, connected to a camera on the roof of the building, which was pointed to the sky. In the middle of the digital pad there were the numbers one through nine in a circle.

"Johnny..."

"Yes, Dad."

"Because this is such a special day, the partners are allowing me to tell you the combination of the lock."

"Seriously? That is so cool."

Johnny and his parents approached the electronic lock and then Mr. Prospect said, "Johnny, the combination is 3-3-3."

"Adds to nine you know Johnny," his mom said in a very playful voice.

Johnny immediately turned and gazed at both of them with questioning eyes and one eyebrow raised. Both of his parents were giving him so many Pimby clues that he just wanted to blurt out "You guys know about Pimbies, right?" But he thought it best to just let the day flow.

His mom then turned to Mr. Prospect and said, "Robert, the number nine is just following Johnny around today. I realized that we were seated in the ninth car, in the ninth row on the train. Isn't that amazing?"

"Yes, it is Desiree, absolutely amazing, almost magical," Mr. Prospect said to his wife while winking at her.

Johnny smiled at them both, not only because they were dropping more Pimby clues, but also because they were both glowing so brightly, and he was so thankful to have them as his parents.

Johnny then entered the combination and as the doors automatically swung open he heard the words "HAPPY BIRTHDAY." Standing behind the doors were Mickey and his parents, Cathy, many more of Johnny's friends and most of his relatives. Johnny was genuinely surprised, and he knew it was because he didn't have expectations about his birthday. He just let it flow.

He stood there, in shock for a few moments, observing all the people and all the different colors shining on him from their chests. As Johnny peered around the room, he realized that all the decorations were orange. He turned to his dad, and before Johnny had time to say anything, his dad picked Johnny up by his waist, raised Johnny above his head and placed him on his shoulders.

Staring up at Johnny, Mr. Prospect smiled and said, "My son, I had a hunch your favorite color was orange."

Glancing down at his dad, Johnny whispered, "YOU KNEW, YOU ALWAYS KNEW."

Still looking up at Johnny, his dad winked at him, put him back down on the ground, and gave him the tightest, strongest hug. His dad then whispered in Johnny's ear, "Yes my son, but I could neither talk to you about it nor be around you often during this time because you had to navigate the journey by yourself. It was your rite of passage, your journey, your experience, and yours alone. I would've been a distraction to you. We have all the time in the world to talk about your journey and help those seeds grow."

"Does Mom know?"

"Yes, she does Johnny, but she'd forgotten about her Pimby and through you and your experiences you changed the balance of energy in the house and your mom was able to reconnect to her imagination. For your birthday, you actually returned the gift of imagination back to your mom."

Johnny's mom looked at him with a tear in her eye, held his hand for a moment and said, "Thank you my son."

Having seen Cathy in the middle of the crowd, Johnny turned back to his father and asked, "Cathy knows for sure right?"

"Yes, Johnny."

"I knew it!"

His parents arranged a magician and a band for the party. During all the events, Johnny slowly made his way around the party to say hello to everyone. Later that morning Johnny and Mickey got a chance to talk alone. Mickey had never been up in the Cloud Club before and was flabbergasted by the view.

"Johnny, this is the coolest place ever. It's really like living on a cloud. It's amazing. This is the best place to have a birthday party!"

"Who knows Mickey, maybe in nine weeks you can have your party here?"

"Yeah, you have to ask your dad about it later," Mickey said while nudging Johnny with his elbow.

All of a sudden Mickey shook his head from side to side and then turned around in a circle.

"What's up Mickey?" Johnny asked.

"Do you hear a humming sound?" Mickey replied.

Johnny started giggling while looking at Mickey.

"What's so funny Johnny? Really dude, I hear humming." Mickey barked at Johnny.

"Nothing. I'm sorry. I wasn't laughing at you. I just remembered that you'll be turning nine in nine weeks."

"What does that have to do with the humming?" Mickey asked while staring at Johnny like he was crazy.

Johnny realized he shouldn't continue the conversation because it had to be Mickey's journey but was unsure how to respond. Then he remembered one of the first times he mentioned the humming to Mickey and so he used Mickey's words to respond and said, "It's just you're getting old, man. You're almost nine and already you're hearing things - or maybe it is because we are up so high."

They started laughing so hard that many of the guests turned to look at them. Johnny and Mickey started pushing each other back and forth in a play fight. They were laughing louder and louder causing them to not pay attention to where they were headed. Nine seconds later Mickey tripped on a rope that was connected to a net of balloons hanging from the ceiling. The net opened and hundreds of party balloons fell to the floor. Everyone started kicking and popping them. Johnny helped Mickey up off the floor and they both looked at the crowd. Johnny observed, at that moment, everyone was having so much fun that they all looked like kids.

Maybe that is what Filbert talked about when he mentioned Einstein and childlike enthusiasm, Johnny thought to himself.

"Did you have fun, Johnny?" his mom asked him after the last of the guests had left the Cloud Club.

"Yes Mom. It couldn't have been better."

"We're so glad you enjoyed it." Mr. Prospect said to Johnny.

Johnny finished one more piece of cake before leaving and as he threw the plate in the garbage, he read the word biodegradable stamped on the back of the plate. He also noticed the cups, napkins, spoons, and forks were marked the same. He asked his parents about it while taking the elevator down to the lobby. They explained to Johnny that the plates were made out of recycled paper and the cups, forks and spoons were made by using corn, potato and soy.

"That's great." Johnny said. It's important to respect the earth."

"As it is to respect your body," said Cathy. "Your body is like your own little earth and that is why you should always take care of yourself. You should always think of your body as a temple," Cathy said winking at Johnny. She then continued to explain that's why she always cooked healthy meals and snacks for the family.

"Exercise is another way to respect your body as well, Johnny," Mrs. Prospect added.

"That's the reason your father and I try to encourage you to be active and not sit in the house all day watching television or playing video games. The earth has given you so much beauty, so many fun places to play and explore, as well as so many ways to use your muscles to strengthen your body, such as riding your bike, climbing trees, swimming, jogging, even yard work is a form of exercise. You were given this body to use Johnny, not to ignore it or let it become weak and frail," said his mom.

She then continued, "Before people had so many machines to do the work for them, such as laundry machines, dishwashers, and power lawnmowers to name a few examples, people had to do many things by hand that allowed them to be in better physical condition than they are today. Today many people, including children, just sit around and are inactive for a large portion of the day. That is one of the many reasons so many people are gaining weight. Johnny, remember to always respect and take care of both the planet and your body, always. Ok?"

"Yes, I promise I will," Johnny replied in a confident and commanding voice, signaling to his family that he was serious to maintain his commitment to respect both his body and the planet.

The four of them slowly walked for hours to the park that afternoon, taking in all the sights and sounds of the city. The sun shone so brightly, but luckily there was a cool breeze. Johnny remembered how hot the city could get and was very thankful for the pleasant breeze. Mr. Prospect had taken a knapsack from his office right before they left, which had a blanket, their lunch and more biodegradable plates and cutlery. They made their way to the spot where they used to picnic when they lived in the city, the same spot Johnny just visited with Filbert.

"Johnny, you have a great memory," Cathy commented. "I can't believe you remembered exactly how to find this spot. You were so young when we all came here for picnics."

"That's true Cathy, but I feel like I was just here recently," Johnny said snickering.

Cathy and his parents laughed with him, understanding it must've had to do with the visits by his Pimby.

After finishing lunch, Johnny laid down on the rock and looked down at the field below.

"Heads up!" Johnny heard from one of the boys on the field.

Johnny turned and watched a soccer ball bounce past him. *Ball*, he thought to himself.

Following lunch, they all went to the lake and rented rowboats. Around 6:30 p.m. they then walked over to the café on the river. The café had a view of the three biggest bridges in the city. That was the first time Johnny realized that bridges had to come from someone's imagination. He'd never seen a bridge built before and thought about how incredible it must've been for the first person to design a bridge without ever having seen one being built before. He truly understood the power of imagination. He knew the engineer must've built the bridge in his imagination first.

I truly do see the world differently now.

They remained to watch the sunset because the west side café had a magnificent view of the sun setting behind all three bridges. As the sun slowly approached the horizon Johnny heard a sound similar to air being let out of a tire. He knew without question that it was the sound of the setting sun. The hissing sound became softer as the sun slowly sank into the horizon. Then the sky began to glow orange and so did Johnny.

Their last destination was Frosty's. The taxi let them off in front of the tallest building in the world. For the first time, Johnny caught that the address was 999 West 18th Street. He turned to his dad who was smiling at him and said, "Are you really surprised Johnny? Yes…nines again."

"I'd never paid attention to the address before, that's so cool. I can't wait to talk to you all about the world of the Pimbies!

"We have so much time for that," Mrs. Prospect said, smiling from ear to ear and glowing so brightly that the whole street was colored pink.

It was 9 p.m. when they arrived at Frosty's and the lights in the city were shining so brightly. Johnny forgot how much more he loved the city at night. He always found it so magical and asked his parents if they could sit by the window.

"Of course," his mom said. "In fact, we reserved the same table we had many years ago."

Johnny smiled. Surprisingly Frosty's hadn't changed one bit in all these years. Johnny thought they might have redecorated by now, but he was incredibly happy they hadn't.

The waiters brought out a huge banana split with four spoons and sparklers in the middle and began singing "Happy Birthday" to Johnny. After they finished, they told Johnny to make a wish. He turned to them and said, "It's already come true, but I guess I can wish that everyone can be this happy." Then his father reached into his knapsack and handed Johnny a gift wrapped in gold foil about the size of a shoebox.

"Mom, Dad, Cathy, this has been the best day ever. You've already given me so much, I don't need another gift," Johnny said in the most grown-up voice his parents had ever heard from him.

"This isn't really a gift Johnny," his father explained, "It's more of a symbol that I've held for you since you were born. It's been in our family for 108 years. My father gave it to me and his to him and so on."

Johnny's hands trembled from holding something so important. Slowly, he unwrapped the present and noticed the box was made from wood. It smelled like cedar and there was a big letter "I" engraved in the center.

Before opening the box, which had three hooks in the front, he asked what the "I" meant.

"Imagination, Johnny, imagination," his dad replied while grinning.

Johnny found a gold kaleidoscope sitting on a cushion of black velvet inside the box. It gleamed just as brightly as his golden temple. He gently picked it up, finding it to be much heavier than it looked. As he rotated it in his hand, he saw that it was dented in a few spots. Carefully, he ran his fingers over the dents and with each dent, to his surprise, he felt tiny electric shocks that ran through his entire body. He immediately closed his eyes and sensed that it was handmade because he could see the old man who made it.

"Dad, sometimes it still seems really weird that these things are happening. Like when I closed my eyes just now, I saw that this was made by a very old man. Do you know who made it?"

"Yes, my son, your great-great-great grandfather."

Johnny was speechless. He continued to hold it for fear of breaking it until his father told him to put it to his eye and point it toward the bright cloud-shaped light in the center of the ceiling at Frosty's. Johnny did as he was told and viewed many magnificent shapes and colors.

Then in a slow deep voice Mr. Prospect said, "Johnny, when my father, your grandfather, gave me the kaleidoscope, he told me that it shows the truth, that it shows the true way to see the world, to see life – always changing with unlimited possibilities."

As Johnny lowered the kaleidoscope from his eye, he slowly looked around the room. To his amazement, he saw light radiating from each person. The room was filled and looked exactly like a kaleidoscope. He then understood what his father was telling him about the kaleidoscope showing the truth, and unlimited possibilities.

Johnny held tightly to the kaleidoscope the whole way home. Mr. Prospect arranged for a taxi to take them back to Hopewell Junction because it was too late to take the train. Johnny stared out the window the whole trip home thinking about all the possibilities that awaited him in life. They arrived home after midnight and Johnny fell asleep as soon as his head hit the pillow.

"Tap-tap."

Johnny turned in his bed annoyed by what sounded like a branch banging against his window.

"Tap-tap-tap."

Again, Johnny turned in his bed, rubbed his eyes and looked at the clock. For a moment he thought maybe Filbert was surprising him with one more visit, but noticed it was 1:54 a.m. He then knew it couldn't be Filbert because he only ever visited at 1:08 a.m.

Johnny let out a big "uffa," punched his pillow making it fluffy, when suddenly he heard something whisper his name.

"What!" he said to himself and walked over to the window.

Down on the lawn below his window he found Mickey staring up, tossing rocks at his house.

"Mickey, are you crazy? What are you doing out so late? We're both going to get in trouble if you wake my parents!" Johnny was yelling down at Mickey in a hushed voice.

"I know Johnny, I know," Mickey said in a panicked voice, "but I had to talk to you."

"You ok Mickey?" Johnny asked trying to hide his worry.

"Yeah Johnny, it's just, well, I saw something outside my window, it freaked me out, you will not believe it. It looked like a …"

Before Mickey could finish his sentence, Johnny said, "I can believe it Mickey. I can believe it!"

From the Author

Thank you for joining me in the land of Pimbies. I truly hope you enjoyed your time with Filbert and Johnny and have found yourself dusted with some Pimby magic. Even better, I hope you've noticed your light radiating with that shimmering piece of imagination we are all gifted with.

We are all blessed with an abundance of opportunities and possibilities. Yet many times we fail to pay attention. The thing is, we must remain open to all the beautiful, precious gems in our life.

Why?

Because those gems color the lens of our kaleidoscope. And the lens through which one views life is the way one will experience life. It is that simple. I say make it joyful and colorful.

Which of the lessons found in this modern-day fable will you choose to color your kaleidoscope? Perhaps to:

- Not fear making a mistake
- Remain flexible
- Let go of expectations and approach life with curiosity
- Rise above negativity and prevent your light from turning grey
- Have a cup of T.E.A every day
- Stop comparing yourself
- Remember there is more than meets the eye – we are all living in rainbow light
- Make room for magic
- Be thankful

My wish is you will forever joyfully stretch like silly putty. That this whimsical journey tickled your imagination and ignited a perspective of wonder.

Your journey has truly just begun.

You are the creative force in your life. Embrace your uniqueness and rise above limitations.

Make your life a daring adventure and as my Grandma Fella told me, **"Live life freely**."

Gratefully yours,

Robert

The creation of something new
is not accomplished by the intellect
but by the play instinct.

Carl Jung

About the Author

Robert is one of those rare individuals who embraces change and lives by a philosophy which he calls Possibility in Action®.

His commitment to empowering readers through intentional living remains unwavering. Through memoirs, life guides, workbooks, and fables, his writings provoke introspection, foster growth, and ignite possibilities. His mission is to empower others to grow their life forward with power and grace.

Born in NYC, Robert has also lived in Abu Dhabi, Dubai, and now lives in Italy. He received his MBA from Columbia University. Formerly a top finance executive, Robert dismantled his life after caring for his late wife with terminal breast cancer to share life lessons. He embraced uncertainty to pursue monumental dreams - a testament to the power of identity shifting.

Robert opted for a new story and now is now a prolific writer, life coach, speaker, and adjunct professor. He embodies the transformational literature he is known for, guiding readers on profound journeys of personal evolution. His impact spans individuals, prestigious organizations, and events globally.

You can learn more about him at his website, www.robertpardi.com or on YouTube @possibilityinaction.

www.ingramcontent.com/pod-product-compliance
Lightning Source LLC
Chambersburg PA
CBHW071506170626
46811CB00007B/2746